Dear Reader,

Welcome to my home, Nashville, Tennessee, the heart of country music.

It was here that I was shaped and nurtured. My granddaddy's religion and my father's fierce love of this land are reflected in my music. And though I've played to sold-out concerts around the world, I always return to my roots. This place restores my spirit.

Of course, my life isn't perfect. One thing's missing.

As far back as I can remember, there was just one thing that mattered more than my music. That was Jordy—Jordan Hunter. From the time she first came to live with my family, I knew I loved that girl with her wide, frightened eyes and that wild mane of gypsy hair. But we both had dreams to chase.

Now she's back, all grown up and in charge of her life. The passion is still there between us. But after all she's been through, she's built a wall around her shattered heart. It's up to me to find a way through that wall if we're ever going to experience the joy of true love.

I wish all of you a dream to chase. And someone special to love the dreamer.

Clint Donner

Tennessee

RUTH LANGAN
To Love a Dreamer

Tennessee

Published by Silhouette Books New York
America's Publisher of Contemporary Romance

To Tom, who took a chance on loving a dreamer

SILHOUETTE BOOKS
300 East 42nd St., New York, N.Y. 10017

TO LOVE A DREAMER

Copyright © 1985 by Ruth Langan

ISBN: 0-373-45192-X

Published Silhouette Books 1985, 1993

Printed in the U.S.A.

Chapter One

"Keep it down! I can't hear my pitch."

"Move that cable out of the way."

"Put that microphone over here."

It was typical backstage chaos before the show. The musicians were setting up their instruments, tuning, testing, feeling the adrenaline begin to pump.

Clint Donner stood to one side of the stage with his drummer, his deep voice low, despite the commotion around him.

"Randy, remember to keep that second number up-tempo. If we draw it out too long, I'm going to have trouble with that low note tonight. I don't mind holding it for a few seconds. After that, I'd like to drop it and go into the chorus."

The dark-bearded drummer nodded.

"And that new song...tell the guys in the band I've decided to go with it. Sooner or later, we have to try it out before an audience. May as well be tonight."

Randy nodded a second time before walking away.

A blond waitress extended her hand, offering Clint a slip of paper. Her jeans looked as if they'd been sprayed on. Her T-shirt, bearing the logo of the barn-size country bar, was at least two sizes too small and clung to her curves like a second skin. She was annoyed that Clint didn't seem to notice.

He read quickly, frowning.

The words were in a still-remembered tidy script:

Clint, I need to see you before you leave town. Strictly business.

Jordan.

His head came up sharply.

"Another note from one of your adoring fans?" The girl rested a round tray against her hip and cracked her gum.

"Where is she sitting?"

The waitress pointed. "About the middle of the room. With six or eight other people."

He scribbled something on the back of the paper, folded it, and handed it back. "See that she gets this."

The blonde sauntered away, hoping he was watching her.

Clint moved quickly to the curtain and peered out. Through the sea of people, he searched carefully until he spotted her. Her back was to him, but there was no mistaking the tiny figure, or the dark hair spilling wild like a Gypsy's down her back.

The band assembled and began the first strains of their opening number. Clint dropped the curtain and walked to the microphone. For the next hour and a half there would be no time to reminisce. No time to think. No time for anger. As the curtain rose, the spotlight found him, smiling, charming, while the audience thundered their approval.

Jordan Hunter turned her chair around so she could face the stage. She had chosen this spot at the table for a reason. Now she could turn her back on the others and lose herself in his music. She didn't want to make conversation, or answer questions. She was content to watch him, to let his voice wash over her, without anyone interrupting her concentration.

As the curtain rose, she felt a sudden sexual pull— an unexpected surge of desire that left her reeling. It had been years since she had felt anything so intense.

Taking a deep breath, she studied him carefully, letting her gaze roam over him slowly. As the spotlight illuminated his features, she drank in the sight of him. The key light gave his thick curly hair a reddish sheen. The back light cast a halo about him. He had a wide forehead, outlined by traces of wayward curls. The face was ruggedly handsome with smooth, even features. The smile was a rogue's smile, warm, but with a hint of danger. If he had lived in another era he would have been a swashbuckling pirate, she thought, riding the waves into danger, then carrying off the bounty, and the beauty, strumming a lute against the night sky.

His piercing eyes were his most outstanding feature. They demanded attention. When he looked at you, it was as if he could see beyond your face, into your very heart.

Clint was a commanding presence, on stage as well as off. But when he was performing, singing those heartrending songs that had given him his fame, he was even bigger than life.

Why are so many country songs about drinking and cheating? she wondered. A lump formed in her throat, threatening to choke her. Because they mirrored life. And that was what so many people faced in their own lives.

The haunting lyrics tore at her, reminding her of old hurts. Not now. Not tonight, she cautioned herself. This was a night for cool reason. Tonight was strictly business.

For over an hour, Jordan sat in the audience, transfixed, caught up in the pure emotion that was always present in Clint's performances. His voice could be smooth as velvet, or raw as whiskey. He sang of his roots, of life's simple pleasures, of joys shared and pain endured. Every song he and the band offered was one he had written himself. The words had special meaning to him, and he shared a part of himself with his audience. He touched them. Like a poet, the songwriter opened his veins, spilling his life's blood on the pages. Every person in the room felt the magic. Clint Donner was the magic.

Jordan pulled herself back to reality and glanced around the darkened room. He was too good for this place. She knew the people loved him, and he returned that affection. That was what kept him doing this, and coming back to the places where he had first been accepted. He was giving back a hundredfold to the people who had first applauded his clumsy attempts to entertain.

But he could do so much more. His voice could tame stadiums filled with raucous fans. With the right people behind him, he could be a superstar.

As he went into his closing number, she groped her way through the dim room and made her way to the bus which sat grumbling like a hulking giant in the darkened parking lot. She knocked, knowing the driver would be aboard. The doors were always locked between performances to keep out any fans bold enough to attempt to sneak on.

The door opened a crack.

"Yeah?"

She handed the note through the opening and waited. Sweat beaded her forehead. The humidity of late September made the night still and close. The heavy Nashville air was sweet with the scent of roses, a scent that always made Jordan think of the farm, and winding country roads, and—Clint. A moment later the door was opened wide enough to allow her to enter. The driver, a book dangling in his left hand, studied her with vague disinterest. The purr of the air conditioner was much louder in here. She breathed in the fresh air, a relief after the room filled with stale tobacco and the heat of a crush of bodies. She made her way to the rear of the vehicle, opening the door to Clint's compartment. When she turned to close the door, the driver was already sprawled on a couch, lost in the book she had obviously interrupted.

There was a tomblike quiet here. It was a little cocoon of privacy where the star could retreat from the public eye. Jordan ran her hand over the sofa that also doubled as a bed. The cushion was mussed. Clint had obviously taken a rest before the show. A pillow was tossed carelessly on the floor. She picked it up and fluffed it before placing it on the sofa.

Along one wall was the stereo system, a television set and a video recording unit. Jordan idly picked up a notepad and studied the familiar scrawl. Clint was working on another song. It would probably be included in his new album, which he and his band would record over the winter months. She studied the notes for a long time, then placed the pad back on the table.

The room was small and compact, and to the casual observer it would look like just another compartment on the bus. But to Jordan, it spoke eloquently of Clint. She could feel him here, smell him, sense his presence.

Without realizing it, she picked up his discarded shirt and held it to her face, breathing in the never-forgotten musky scent of him. Closing her eyes, she could imagine him hovering near.

Or was it just imagination? Dropping the shirt, she turned, as if drawn by a magnet. He closed the door as softly as he had opened it, and leaned against it, those intense eyes studying her, piercing her very soul.

* * *

Clint realized that he had been holding his breath, waiting for a glimpse of her face. He expelled his breath slowly. They were the same lovely features he would always remember. Eyes so green they glowed like liquid emeralds. Lips pursed into a tiny pout, the lower lip full, sensuous. High cheekbones that gave her face a mysterious, exotic quality. And that wild, dark hair that drifted softly about her face and shoulders, nearly to her waist.

A sudden smile suffused her features with warmth and light.

"Clint." She took a quick step forward, then stopped, suddenly awkward.

Up close, he noticed the satin gloss of her skin, as smooth as a child's. She was wearing almost no makeup. Thick dark lashes fluttered as her eyes crinkled into the most beguiling smile.

"Hello Jordy." He folded his arms across his chest, to keep from opening them wide and gathering her close.

She noticed the stiff posture, and the smile faded.

"Sit down." He gestured to the only chair, and she sat quickly.

Clint leaned his guitar against the end of the sofa and sat down, his long legs stretched out lazily before him.

"It was a great show, Clint. As always. You keep getting better."

He offered a faint smile. "Thanks. Now, what's this note about business?"

She bit her lip. It was obvious he intended to keep it brief.

"I know you're leaving on a tour."

He nodded. "Marty set it up, before he..." He gestured with a hand, as if to dismiss the word he avoided. "We'll be gone a month. We leave tonight."

She caught her breath. Even less time than she had thought.

"I see. Tonight." She paused, then took the plunge. "I know you chose to honor the contract you had with Marty. I appreciate it, Clint. I also know the contract is up, and that you've put out the word that you're interviewing for a new manager."

He nodded. "So?"

"So, I'd like to interview."

He started to stand. "Come on, Jordy. Be serious."

She thrust a card into his hand. "The name isn't Jordy. It's J. D. Hunter now. And I am being serious. I've decided to quit my job with the record company and take over Marty's business full-time."

"Why?"

She noticed with relief that he sat back down, and after a cursory examination of the business card, gave her his full attention.

"Because there's no future with the record company. Because I know all about Marty's business. Long before he died, I had been doing some of the work." She licked her lips, knowing she could say a lot more. She resisted the urge to tell him everything. "I have the qualities necessary to be a manager—honesty, dedication, an ability to get things organized."

She spoke quickly, hoping to sway him before he lost patience. "I'm a nurturing kind of person. Marty always said that was important, if you wanted to manage a band. I'd be willing to take care of you, of all the guys in the band, the way you should be taken care of. I'd mother you. Care about you. Put your needs first. I'd see to all the little details that I think have been overlooked for too long now. Also, Clint, I have a lot of contacts in the record industry. Especially in the publicity departments. That's to your advantage when I'm setting up interviews and appearances.''

She held up her fingers, ticking off the rest. "I'm good with figures. I'll take care of your books. I know you hate that," she added with a nervous laugh. "I'll see to paying the bills." She folded down another finger. "I'll even make sure you have someone backstage with a towel after every performance." She had noticed that lapse on her way to the bus. She watched him brush away the last traces of sweat, and met his look with a knowing smile. "What do you say?"

"I'd say you've been doing your homework, Jordy." He leaned back, studying her so closely she flushed. "Do you need money?"

The question caught her by surprise.

"I'm fine."

"Umm." He saw her look down suddenly. "I've been hearing some rumors, Jordy. Marty died without insurance, didn't he?"

She licked her lips. "Yes."

"And I understand he left a lot of unpaid bills as well."

"They're all paid now, Clint."

Wearily he rubbed the back of his neck in a familiar gesture. "I already have a lot of people to look out for, Jordy. I don't think I want to take on any more responsibilities."

He saw the green eyes blaze. "I'm not asking you to take care of me, Clint." She stood and turned her back on him, but he watched her hands clench at her sides. "I've been taking care of myself for a long time." Almost to herself, she added, "My God, sometimes it seems like forever." Louder she said, "All I want is the chance to prove that I can be a good manager. Better than Marty, if you want to know the truth."

He studied her rigid back for long, silent moments, reminding himself that the exquisite creature standing there was a woman, not a child. His shoulders lifted as he took in a strong, deep breath. She had defeated him before she'd even started, but he wouldn't let her know that.

"All right. We'll try it for six months. But I'm going to work you to death. These last months have been a mess. You'll have to start at the very bottom. Get together with our road manager, correlate all our concert dates, set up whatever publicity you can. Show me your stuff, Jordy, and if you're as good as you say, we'll talk about a contract."

She turned a solemn face to him.

"Deal?" He offered his hand.

She stared at the hand for a moment, then gave him the benefit of a smile. "Deal. You won't regret it, Clint."

"No. But you may."

As their hands touched, she felt tremors that started at her fingertips and shot all the way through her body. A jolt of lightning would have been less startling. She pulled her hand away, rubbing it on the leg of her jeans.

He opened the door. "I'll see you in a month."

"Your name will be in so many magazines and newspapers by then, you'll think you're running for president."

He chuckled, and she remembered how much she loved the sound of his laughter. "Make sure they spell my name right."

He watched as she made her way down the aisle of the bus, chatting and joking with the guys in the band. He remembered with a start that she was twenty-three, older than two of his band members.

When at last he closed the door of his compartment, he picked up his guitar and sat down in the chair she had vacated.

Her perfume still lingered. Idly strumming the instrument, he closed his eyes, inhaling the soft, womanly scent of her, and the memories, so long held at bay, rushed back.

She had been thirteen the first time he saw her. Alone in the world, and probably terrified. The first thing he noticed were green eyes that looked enormous in that delicate face. Waist-length dark hair drifted around her shoulders like an opaque veil. She had paused on the threshold of their big, old sprawling house, looking like a fawn from the forest, about to bolt. He and his three brothers had faced her in silence.

His mother dropped a protective arm about her shoulders, while his father cleared his throat and rumbled, "Boys, this is Jordan. She and her folks moved into the Higgins place last year, while you were away at school. Their house burned. Her folks have died and she's going to live with us a while. See that you watch out real carefully for her."

And that was it. Except for the normal questions and explanations, there was acceptance. From then on, Jordy had been treated as part of the family.

His mother had always wanted a daughter, and she probably saw it as fate when the neighbor's child was left alone in the world. But in less than a year his mother was gone, and Jordan found herself alone in the big old farmhouse with only Clint's father. The sons were away at college, or already on their own. Fifteen years older than his wife, and badly slowed by a stroke, Clint's father required constant care until his death. It all fell to Jordy.

Clint joined the service, and afterward began singing with a band. He was gone for weeks and months at a time, missing most of her growing up years, seeming not to notice that she was becoming a woman. Even now, he realized, she looked more like that wild little girl than a woman.

He frowned. On her sixteenth birthday, he had watched her blow out the candles of her cake and make a wish. She had turned to him then and whispered, "Will you wait for me, Clint?"

His brothers had laughed at her innocent question. But the joke was on him. A sudden look of pain crossed his face. She was the one who hadn't waited.

With an angry gesture, he dropped the guitar and put on the earphones to his stereo. Turning up the volume, he leaned back in the chair, determined to blot out all thought.

Jordan's feet fairly flew to her car. She had done it. Tomorrow, she would give her notice at work.

She slammed the door and sat in the darkened automobile, mentally checking off all the things she would have to do before Clint got back from his tour. Arrange an interview with one of the major trade magazines. A few radio interviews. And at least one record promo. She'd start phoning first thing in the morning.

Working in the record industry, she had made a lot of connections. And there were a few debts owed her. Now she would call in those debts, and start making Clint Donner's name a household word.

She started the car and drove slowly toward her apartment in downtown Nashville. She had given up the big apartment she and Marty had leased. She had sold his luxury car too. This used model was on its last leg. But at least it provided transportation. Right now, this minute, nothing mattered except the fact that she had convinced Clint to give her a chance. The rest would be up to her.

She let herself into the darkened apartment and switched on the light. An old poster of Clint, taken three years earlier, stared at her from the wall over her kitchen table. She studied the dark eyes, which seemed to watch her as she passed by. She remembered hanging that poster to celebrate.

When Marty had come home that day to tell her he had gotten the job as Clint's manager, she had been speechless. She and Marty both held down jobs at a local record company, and Marty had boasted that he could do better. She never did know how he had managed to talk himself into the position of manager, but she wasn't about to question fate. They needed the money. Marty spent it faster than both of them could manage to earn it.

She had never met a man who could talk a better game than Marty Hunter. He was the quintessential salesman. A silver-tongued devil. Hadn't he sold her on the idea of marriage less than a week after she had met him? Hadn't he kept her dangling with promises of better times, a better life, if only she would hang on and give him time to find his big break? She never questioned how he had talked his way into being Clint's manager. If anyone could do it, Marty could.

Jordan set the kettle on the stove, and pulled off her jeans and cotton shirt. After pulling on an oversize football jersey, she hung her clothes in the cramped closet and made herself some instant coffee.

She turned down the sheets of her bed and snuggled against the pillow, resting the coffee on her lap. A small smile played on her lips. She was so relieved that she had swayed Clint without having to tell him the whole story. What would he think if he found out his manager hadn't been able to do his work for almost the last eight months of his contract, that she had actually done the bulk of the work?

Jordan took a long swallow of hot coffee, then leaned her head back. She had covered for Marty, trying to keep it all together. She had managed her own job, and Marty's too. But it had taken its toll. Sometimes she'd wondered how she managed to crawl out of bed in the mornings. And when word of Marty's accident reached her, she had watched like someone in a dream while her world crumbled around her. Even now, there were times she awoke in a cold sweat, wondering if she had the strength to keep going.

Now, at least, the mountain of debts had been whittled and she would be doing only one job—the one she had always wanted to do.

Hot coffee sloshed over the rim of the cup, burning through her nightshirt.

Swearing under her breath, she jumped up and ran for a towel. Tears burned her eyelids, and she impatiently brushed them away as she mopped up the hot liquid.

Angrily dumping the rest of the contents in the sink, she snapped off the light and climbed into bed.

She knew she wasn't crying over the coffee, or the burn. And she wasn't crying over a husband who had died almost a year ago.

Odd, she almost never cried. But tonight, she knew, she was shedding tears over something that had been dead even longer.

She turned her face into the pillow, and swallowed back the tears. She was crying over a lost dream. A lousy childish fantasy. And it wasn't worth crying over. Dreams weren't for the common man. Dreams were for poets, and songwriters—and singers strong enough to keep on chasing the dream.

Chapter Two

"**W**hat in the hell . . . ?"

Clint stood just inside the door of the tiny office, his hand on the knob. All around him lay boxes of paper, file folders, an unconnected telephone, a battered typewriter.

Jordan was perched on a stepladder, attempting to fasten a shade to the window.

Her faded jeans had a hole in one knee. The sleeves of her cotton shirt were rolled above her elbows. She had twisted her long hair into one fat braid which fell forward over her shoulder.

"Clint! You weren't due in for hours." Her eyes widened. For a moment, she looked as if she would pitch forward. Then, clutching the top of the ladder, she righted herself.

Tapered jeans accented Clint's long legs and lean hips. The casual Western shirt couldn't camouflage the corded muscles of his arms and shoulders. His hair was a bit shaggy, but on him, she thought, it looked wonderful. He seemed weary. A month on the road was a long time.

Quickly composing herself, she climbed down, unaware that her face bore the smudges of her morning's work.

"Well? What do you think?" She spread her arms to encompass the cramped quarters.

"How much is this costing me?" He studied the tiny streaks of dirt parading across her nose and one cheek, and resisted the urge to wipe them away.

"It was a steal. And they threw in the desk and file cabinet. All I had to do was clean it, and pay three months' rent in advance."

He realized she had evaded his question.

"How much, Jordy?"

"Four hundred a month." She sneaked a quick look before turning away.

"A hundred dollars a week for this hole-in-the-wall!"

"I told you, Clint. They threw in the desk and..."

"Yes. I heard you. The desk and file cabinet. Why do you need this, Jordy? Why can't you work out of your own place?"

She flushed and sat down behind the desk, hoping it gave her a look of authority. "I've set up a couple of interviews. They wanted to come to the office. I couldn't very well tell them we didn't have an office."

"All you had to do was invite them to your apartment. Would that be so difficult?"

She folded her hands on top of the desk, and met his dark gaze. "I don't have the two-bedroom apartment anymore." She licked her lips. "I decided it was too big for just me. I took a walk-up downtown."

His anger dissolved. He couldn't bear to call her bluff. It was better if he pretended to be ignorant of her financial situation.

"Okay." He sat down in the rickety chair opposite her desk. "Give me a rundown on the schedule you've put together."

She pulled a list from the desk drawer. With one hand, she flicked the braid behind her. "Tomorrow, you have an interview at eleven o'clock with a reporter and photographer from *Country Roads Magazine*."

She heard him curse and looked up. "Something wrong?"

"I wanted to drive out to the farm tomorrow. It's been a long month."

"Can't it wait until the day after?"

"I guess it will have to." He idly tapped a finger on the arm of the chair. "What else?"

"Saturday afternoon, I've set up a record promotion at a local mall."

"Saturday? Come on, Jordy. Do you know what those things are like?"

"Of course I do. That used to be my business, remember?" In a more patient tone, she explained, "Sales have been way down in the mall. The record store was thrilled to hear that you'd come in and autograph for an hour. And it certainly won't hurt your career either. That is my primary concern, Clint."

"It'll be a mob scene. You know how I hate that sort of thing."

"That's the price one pays for fame," she said, with the barest hint of a smile playing at her lips.

"Damn it, Jordy." He stood in agitation. "I just came in from a hard month on the road. I need some time to myself."

"After tomorrow, you can drive up to the farm and stay until the weekend." She walked up beside him, and for a moment, forgot herself and touched his arm. "Can't you hold out for one more day?"

He stared down at the hand on his arm as if it repelled him. Embarrassed, she dropped it abruptly to her side and took a step back.

An awkward silence stretched between them. Clint was the first to break it.

"I guess I have no choice."

He strode to the door. With his hand on the knob he turned. "I wish you had checked these dates with me before you committed me to them."

"You were on the road. Besides, it's my job to see to your publicity. All you have to do is go along and charm your adoring public."

"Before you go out in public, you'd better wash your face, Jordy. I'd hate to have my fans disillusioned by thinking I hired a little kid to be my manager."

As her mouth dropped open, he added in his sweetest tone, "Have a nice day."

At his retreating back, she hissed, "The same to you."

While the photographer snapped roll after roll of film, the auto wind of his camera whirred in the background. The eager young journalist scribbled furiously, afraid to miss a single word.

Clint had been no help at all, resorting to an incoherent mumble after the reporter asked whether he was disappointed in the sales of his last album.

Jordan forced a bright smile. Her voice rose. "He's my father, my brother, my best friend. We tell each other everything. I even help him pick out his clothes."

At this frank admission, the reporter glanced up a moment at Jordan, then shot a sideways glance at the ominously quiet Clint, before commenting, "You make it sound as if you do everything a wife would do."

"That's right. Everything except sleep with him."

The journalist beamed at that scandalous slip and bent to her notebook, completely missing the murderous scowl that Clint shot at Jordan.

"Have you ever been tempted to...you know...?"

Jordan folded her hands primly on the desk top. "Sleep with him?" She gave a derisive laugh. "I don't think Clint Donner needs any help in that department."

The reporter was practically chuckling in glee at the way this interview had gone. Finally snapping her notebook shut, she stood and extended her hand.

"Thanks, Mrs. Hunter."

"J.D," Jordan corrected.

"Right. Thanks, J.D." She turned, extending her hand to the singer. "And I really appreciate the time you gave me, Mr. Donner."

"Clint," Jordan insisted before he could speak.

"Yes. This was a terrific interview. Thanks, Clint."

He shook her hand. "You're welcome."

The reporter stuffed her notebook into her oversize shoulder bag and followed the photographer from the cramped office.

When the door closed behind them, Clint exploded.

"What the hell was that all about? Jordy, I can't believe you'd say such stupid things to a reporter from *Country Roads Magazine*. Don't you realize what kind of gossip will be flying around by tomorrow? She'll have a field day with this one."

Cool green eyes appraised the tall figure towering over her desk. "It's certainly better than what she had picked up on earlier."

Late-afternoon sunlight slanted through the smudged windows of the office, touching his shaggy hair with red highlights. Piercing dark eyes met and held hers, demanding an explanation.

"You missed the point completely, didn't you?" Her voice took on the tone of a lecturer. "My telecom instructor taught me something important nearly a year ago, Clint. He said that every reporter likes to pick up on one thing he thinks is important, and play that up as the lead in an interview. If that lead is negative, the trick is to feed something less important to the interviewer, and make him think it's the key item."

He interrupted. "Your telecom instructor?"

"Telecommunications. Night classes at the local university extension. I've been going for years to catch up on what I missed."

He grew silent.

Her voice lowered. "In case you hadn't noticed, that eager-beaver reporter came in here determined to play up the poor sales of your last album. If I hadn't come up with something juicier, something that would get her off the track, that would have been her lead in the article."

She spread her hands in a gesture of appeal. "Can I help it if most of her readers would rather speculate on our... relationship, than on the amount of money you make on album sales?"

Angry dark eyes studied her in silence for long minutes.

She was a puzzle. Today, there was no trace of the little girl. The wild tangle of hair had been tamed into a sophisticated knot at her nape. Dressed in a dark, tailored suit and simple white blouse, her face carefully made-up, she gave the perfect impression of a streetwise, knowledgeable business woman who had taken over her late husband's management contract with the ease of a veteran. When his portion of the interview had floundered, Clint had watched with awe as she had assessed the situation and took control.

He expelled his breath. "You'd better be right about this, Jordy. You know how I hate these things. If you've miscalculated..."

"You'll just have to trust me, Clint."

She froze at the icy look that crossed his face. A moment later, she wondered if she had been mistaken. He forced a smile.

"Come on, Jordy. I'm hungry. Let's have some lunch."

She pulled her purse from a desk drawer. "Good. I'm starving."

"There's a diner just down the street that makes the best homemade soup in town. Want to try it?" He opened the door, and heard it squeak. He made a mental note to bring some oil along on his next visit. The sound of that door must drive her crazy.

She nodded. "I've already discovered the diner. I practically live there. It's become my home away from home." As she hurried to keep up with his loose, easy strides, she added, "The kitchen in my place is pretty small. So it's easier to just grab something here in the diner."

He slowed his walk to accommodate her shorter strides. Glancing at her happy smile, he realized just how much he enjoyed the sound of her voice.

As they entered the diner, the wonderful smell of onions on the grill welcomed them.

The old man behind the counter turned with a smile.

"Hi, Will."

"Hey, Jordan. Good to see you."

"What's the soup today?"

"Beef. With lots of noodles."

"Did you bake any bread?"

He nodded. "Wheat."

"Great." As they sat down, Jordan said, "Will, this is Clint Donner."

"Hey, Clint. How're you doing?" He slapped him on the shoulder and winked at her. "I've known Clint since he was a pup."

She was surprised. "He's my boss you know."

Will raised an eyebrow. "That so?"

She nodded, then turned to Clint. "Want the soup?"

He grinned at Will. "Whatever she's having." To Jordan, he added, "You did tell me to trust you, didn't you?"

"Coming up." The old man set two steaming bowls before them.

They sat at the counter on old wooden stools, worn smooth from years of use. While they enjoyed the meal, Will kept up a running conversation, quizzing Clint about his brothers and about his career.

"I hear your brother Glen is a big-city lawyer now."

Clint nodded. "Set up his practice in Knoxville. He's doing fine."

"Thinking about going into politics, is he?"

Clint evaded the question. "He hasn't said. Could be."

"Wouldn't hurt to have a famous singer in the family, would it?"

Clint chuckled. "Nope. Wouldn't hurt a bit."

"What about your brother Earl?"

"He married a girl from Overton County. They have a big old spread up there. About two hundred acres."

The old man arched his eyebrows in approval. "Good for him. What about your brother Danny? I heard he had to drop out of medical school."

"No. He thought about quitting for a while, until he'd earned enough to finish. But he...came into some money just in time."

Jordan watched Clint's face as he spoke. The real affection he felt for his brothers was evident in his soft smile, the inflection of his words.

"Did Danny become a big-city doctor?"

Clint grinned. "That's not Danny's style. He's a country doctor. That's all he ever wanted to be. He's got a thriving practice in De Kalb County."

"You be sure you tell them Old Will asked about them." The old man watched in open admiration as Clint paid the bill and walked to the door.

When they left the diner, Clint asked, "Would you mind driving me to my apartment, Jordy? I had my driver drop me at your office."

"No problem." She led him back down the street toward the office.

As she opened the door of her car, Clint stared. "What happened to the sports car Marty had?"

She climbed in, avoiding his eyes. "I sold it."

He sat down beside her, tucking his long legs carefully into the cramped quarters. With a grin, he studied her as she tried to start the car.

"Are you sure this thing will run?"

She pumped the gas pedal several times, then tried again, holding her breath until it caught. "It gets me where I need to go. It's just a little moody." She turned to him with a half smile. "Like some people I know."

He noticed the portable tape player on the seat between them. As she followed his directions, he pushed the Start button, and heard a song from his latest album.

"You have great taste in music, Jordy."

She laughed. "And you, Mr. Donner, have a giant ego."

"Turn right up ahead. I'm staying in Belle Meade."

While she drove, with his music playing in the background, Clint turned to watch her. Little wisps of hair had already come loose from the neat knot, trailing long tendrils of dark silk along her neck.

She turned the car into a wide, tree-shaded section of town, where million-dollar houses had been built on rolling acres. The well-kept lawns and manicured gardens exuded success, wealth, culture.

Clint pointed to an antebellum mansion of red brick, with huge white pillars. "This is where I'm staying."

She shot him a meaningful glance.

At his lazy grin, her heart trembled. "It belongs to a friend in the business who's currently doing an Australian tour."

"Some friend. This isn't exactly like loaning you his car."

"Well, I do pay some rent. And a place like this is safer with someone living in it."

"He must be a good friend to trust you with his mansion."

"She is."

Jordan's heart fell. She turned to find him studying her carefully. His arm rested along the back of the seat. His fingers caught a loose strand of hair, and he absently twisted it, feeling the silky texture.

"Would you like to go up to the farm with me for a few days, Jordy?"

She hadn't been back to his family farm in years. She held her breath for a moment, caught by surprise. She met his dark gaze, wondering what he was thinking. She could read nothing from his expression.

She was completely unaware of the look that had come into her own eyes at his question. Her face, and especially her eyes, were so expressive, it was easy to tell that she had been caught off guard by his invitation.

"No, Clint. I have a lot to do before the record promo on Saturday."

"There's a telephone at the farm. You can handle everything from there."

She licked her lips, then looked away. His fingers still clutched the strand of her hair, and she wondered if he knew what his touch was doing to her nerves.

"No. But thanks anyway. Have a good rest."

She tried to pull back, but his fingers tightened on her hair, holding her still. Her frightened gaze was imprisoned by the commanding look in his eyes.

"Last month you said you were a nurturing person. Today you told that young reporter you took such good care of me, you were practically a wife. Was it all talk, Jordy?"

His voice had lowered dangerously. She found her gaze drawn to his mouth.

"I do talk a pretty good game. But I also think we both know what my duties are, Clint. Accompanying you to the farm isn't one of them.'' Her voice dropped to a whisper. ''Neither is sleeping with you.''

He studied the dark strand of hair, avoiding her eyes. ''You're right, Jordy.'' He let go of her and opened the car door.

She added in her most saccharine tone, ''I'm sure there are dozens of women who'd love to spend a few days helping you recover from a grueling month on the road.''

He stepped from the car and ducked his head down. ''Right again, Jordy.'' His dark eyes pinned her. ''I'll see you Saturday, at the mall.''

She turned the key, grateful that the car started on the first attempt. As she drove away, she could see Clint in the rearview mirror, standing where she had left him, watching her until she turned the corner of the sleek drive.

Jordan slogged through the rain of the parking lot. She had been unable to find her umbrella. Wisps of hair frizzed softly about her face. She didn't see the puddle until she had stepped in it. Water washed over the open toes of her sandals.

The early November day was as dreary as her mood. She leaped over a second puddle, then darted for the sliding doors of the mall.

Inside, she shook the water from her hair, slipped off the slicker that covered her red shirtwaist dress and moved through the crowds of shoppers.

She hadn't heard from Clint since Tuesday, when he'd left for his family farm, about a hundred miles from Nashville. By now he should be sufficiently rested and ready to take on the mobs of fans waiting impatiently at the record shop.

As she entered the store, she felt her hopes rise slightly. At least there was a good crowd. She knew Clint hated this sort of thing, but he didn't realize how much worse it would be if no one bothered to show up.

Spotting the manager, she fixed a smile on her face. "Good crowd."

The manager nodded. "Great crowd. If this keeps up, we're going to have a sellout on our hands."

He held out his hand. "Why don't I take your raincoat to the back room."

She handed it over.

"Want some coffee?"

She shook her head. "No thanks. Where do you want Clint to sit while he autographs the albums?"

"We have a table back there."

She followed the direction of his hand. "I think you should move it closer to the entrance. That way, people passing by will spot him and be enticed to come in."

The manager looked at her with new respect. "You've got a point, J.D. All right, I'll have one of my employees move it closer."

He glanced at his watch. "He wouldn't be late, would he?"

"Never. Clint Donner is the complete professional. Don't worry, he'll be right on time."

As the manager walked away, Jordan found herself crossing her fingers. If Clint showed up late, she'd personally murder him.

At exactly two o'clock, Jordan heard squeals of feminine excitement from the direction of the entrance. A few moments later, Clint strode into the record shop. His presence filled the store. The crowd hushed, then exploded into sound. An unruly line began forming around the table, with hands reaching over heads, trying to be first to hand him an album to sign.

Immediately, Jordan took his arm and showed him to his chair. "Glad you're prompt," she whispered. "Don't do anything until we get them under control."

With the help of the manager and several employees, Jordan assembled the mob into a fairly orderly line. Only then did she give Clint the word to begin the autographing.

After the first half hour of chaos, she was able to relax and watch Clint at work.

He was more than a professional. To these people, he was a chronicler of their lives. He was friend and neighbor. Besides signing his name, he obliged the fans by penning personal messages they requested, and offering kisses to those bold enough to ask.

Jordan watched the look of adoration on the faces of his fans. He had such wide appeal, from teens to grandmothers. She was aware that there were a lot of men in the line as well, some requesting notes to wives and girlfriends, others shaking his hand, telling him how much his songs meant to them. She watched his face as he spoke with the crowd. There was no pretense now. He was thoroughly enjoying his close contact with these people.

Jordan relaxed, and walked to the back room for a cup of coffee. She felt vindicated. Seeing how angry he had been when she first mentioned this appearance, she had worried that it had been a mistake. Now, she realized that her first instincts had been correct. This sort of exposure was good for Clint's career. But it was also good for Clint personally. He needed to stay in touch with his audience. He needed to hear how much they loved his songs. For the dreamer and poet in him, this was essential.

Even though she had told Clint the appearance would only take an hour, she had promised the record shop manager two hours of Clint's time. Watching the throngs, Jordan decided to extend the time by another hour. When that time was up, she shot a glance at Clint's face, and realized he had had enough.

Motioning the manager aside, she suggested he begin to move the crowd back.

"I can't. They won't be budged."

Jordan thought a minute. "All right. How many albums are left on the shelf?"

He returned a minute later. "They're all gone."

"Good. Promise the rest of the people that if they leave their names, Clint will personally autograph albums for them when you get more in from the record company. That way, you're guaranteed the sales, and they're not disappointed that you ran out of records."

It took nearly another hour before the crowd thinned to the point that Jordan could politely extract Clint from the store.

Dusk had settled. The myriad lights of the parking lot were glinting in the puddles, but the rain had almost stopped.

He made a face and flexed his hand. "Writer's cramp."

"I'm sorry, Clint." Her voice lowered. "I should have found a way to get you out of there sooner. I could see that you were getting tired. I'll get better at this as we do it more often."

He turned to face her, and pulled up the collar of her slicker. Catching a handful of hair, he tucked it inside the collar, to keep it dry. It was an intimate gesture that sent a tiny ripple along her spine.

"No need to apologize, Jordy. You did just fine. In fact, I'm glad now that you set this up. I enjoyed meeting the people."

He smiled down into her face and brushed a raindrop from her lashes. "Join me for dinner. I know a great spot."

Before she could answer, he caught her hand and moved toward his car.

"But my car is over there," she protested.

"We'll get it later."

She found herself nearly running to keep up with his impatient strides.

The restaurant in Printer's Alley was small and elegant, the lighting dim enough to assure privacy. The maître d' smiled his welcome at Clint, and quickly found him a secluded booth. The waiter and busboy fussed over them, seeing to their smallest request.

Jordan sipped the wine Clint had ordered, and smiled in appreciation.

"You look rested, Clint. Ready for some heavy-duty publicity appearances?"

He stretched his long legs and smiled at her. Again she was struck by the hint of danger in that smile.

"Sure, Jordy. Are you going to be with me?"

"Of course. I set them up. I expect to see that everything goes as planned."

"Then how can I miss?"

There was a companionable silence as they enjoyed their meal. Jordan was famished, since she had been too nervous to eat all day. She hoped this nervousness didn't last much longer. Already, her clothes were beginning to show her weight loss.

As she sipped coffee, and Clint enjoyed an after-dinner brandy, he studied her in the dim light. "You look tired, Jordy. Have you been getting enough sleep?"

She flushed. She couldn't remember the last time someone had worried about her.

"I'm fine, Clint. It's just the excitement of the new job. I'll settle down." She studied him over the rim of her cup. "How about you? Did you get a chance to rest at the farm?"

"Umm. It was good. I got a chance to take the dogs out hunting. Did a lot of walking. Worked on a few new song lyrics. Listened to nature. I need that every so often."

He reached his hand across the table, resting it on hers. She forced herself not to pull away, even though she could feel the tremors begin.

She looked up to see his gaze burning over her face. His thumb traced her fingers, then pressed the pulse-beat at her wrist.

Abruptly, he signaled the waiter for the check.

They rode back to the parking lot in silence, the radio playing softly in the background.

When they reached the now-deserted mall, Clint held the door for Jordan while his car idled.

Before she climbed into her car, she turned with a small smile. "Thanks for dinner, Clint. I'll see you on Tuesday. We have a radio interview at seven in the morning. That should reach a big audience. Everyone driving to work will be listening."

The rain had stopped completely, leaving a fine mist. It gleamed like diamonds in her dark hair, and matted her eyelashes.

With his thumb and finger, Clint caught her chin and tilted it.

His voice was husky. "God, Jordy, you're lovely."

She swallowed, too stunned to speak. It wasn't at all what she had expected.

She blinked, then stared into his dark eyes, seeing herself reflected there. What did he see in her eyes? she wondered. She mustn't show him what she really felt.

As if reading her thoughts, he murmured, "Sorry. That was out of line, wasn't it?"

Although he broke contact, and dropped his hand to his side, he continued to stand just inches from her, staring down into her eyes, his lips hovering just above hers, as if unwilling to break the spell completely.

It would be so easy to stand on tiptoe and touch her lips to his. She knew that if she did, his arms would come around her, and he would hold her close to his chest. It was inevitable. And so tempting. For just a few minutes, she could pretend they were lovers, and she could relax against him, drawing on his strength, feeling his warmth.

He watched the range of emotions crossing her features, and cautioned himself not to rush her.

Denying temptation, she turned and yanked open the door to her old car. Settling herself inside, she glanced up at him.

"Good night, Clint."

"'Night, Jordy."

He waited until her car started and the headlights moved away across the parking lot before climbing into his own car. He drove mechanically, his mind still on the bewitching woman who had just left him, alone and empty—again.

Chapter Three

The holidays sped past in a blur of work. Jordan hadn't been so busy, or felt so fulfilled in years. She kept meticulous records for the accountant. Every bill the band incurred was paid on time. She saw to the smallest detail when the band had an engagement, even keeping her promise that someone backstage would have towels for them when the performance ended. If their engagement was too far from town for her to attend personally, she arranged for someone to take care of the little details.

She called in debts from record companies and contacted every publicity department she could. The single phone line had been replaced with a push-button phone and three lines. She still ran the office alone, doing all the typing and phoning herself, and then poring over the bills in her evening hours.

She had become accustomed to having Clint drop by the office whenever he was in town. Without realizing it, she began to look forward to his company. He would slump down in the chair across from her desk, his long legs stretched out in front of him, his chin resting on his folded hands, watching, listening as she persuaded record company executives and producers of talk shows to meet with her employer.

It was the quiet, expectant winter season in Nashville. With country fairs and open-air concerts out of the way, most of the bands were preparing for recording sessions.

Clint had become moody and irritable, retreating for long days to the deserted family farm. As always, he was unhappy with the way his songwriting was going, and, like a true poet, ready to throw away everything he had written and start over.

His mood was contagious. The members of the band became jumpy, especially when they had to spend long hours together confined in the bus. Small arguments broke out, threatening to become major fights if someone didn't work overtime smoothing the wrinkles.

To Jordan's consternation, she discovered that this too was her realm. The more irritable and withdrawn Clint became, the more she worked overtime to soothe him, for the others' sake as well as his own.

It was a Monday morning, nearly noon, when she heard the growl of the bus. A moment later Clint's familiar, lean figure stood in the doorway to her office.

As always, her heart leaped at the sight of him. And as always, she strove to keep her feelings from showing.

"Hi." She gave him a wide smile. "Good gig?"

He leaned against the door, his dark eyes lingering on her.

"It was O.K."

He sat down, still watching her.

"I think I've got you on the *Weekend Report.* The producer is going to get back to me in a little while."

"No." His voice was so low, she looked up in surprise.

"What?"

"I said no." He folded his hands across his chest and watched her.

"Clint, you can't be serious. Do you know how long I've..."

"No more, Jordy. We're recording in less than a month. And I still don't have some of the songs the way I want them."

"But..."

"I want you to cut back on all the publicity until after the recording session. It's bad enough that we still have to fulfill some engagements while we're recording."

She recognized that tone of voice. It revealed his utter exhaustion. There was also a wariness, as if he were watching her reaction. What he needed now was some solitude, some distance from the crowds that were closing in.

"All right, Clint. No more appearances until after the recording session."

He stood. The weariness showed in the slump of his shoulders, on his taut features. For one brief second, she longed to put her arms around him and hold him. He looked defeated.

The phone rang, and she picked it up mechanically, still studying him. While she spoke to a faceless voice, he turned and walked from the office.

She had put in a long day. When the door opened, her eyes jerked up from the bills she was totaling. Once again, Clint stood outlined in the doorway. She was surprised to note that it was dark outside.

"Don't you ever go home?" His voice was a low growl.

"I...got too busy to notice the time." She flipped the papers into a desk drawer. "What's wrong, Clint?"

"I tried calling you at your apartment. When you didn't answer, I got a little concerned."

"You didn't have to drive all the way over here." She studied him as he leaned against the door, his lazy stance belying the tension she could feel clear across the room. "Why didn't you just call here? Then you would have known I was all right."

"I needed to see for myself."

She shrugged. "Well, now you see."

He continued to stand by the door. "Have you eaten?"

She thought about it. "Not since breakfast."

"Come on. I'll buy you dinner."

She stood. "I'm not dressed for dinner."

His gaze roamed over her narrow jeans and cotton shirt, lingering on the soft swell of her breasts. She felt the heat rise to her cheeks.

"What's wrong with the way you're dressed?"

"Nothing... for this place, where no one ever sees me." Her voice held a hint of derisive laughter. "But I can't go to a restaurant like this."

"Then I'll buy you pizza and beer." He held out his hand. "Come on. I know a great pizza joint."

As their fingers joined, she wondered if he ever felt the sudden jolt that she always experienced when they touched. She stole a glance at his face as they walked through the doorway. She could read nothing there.

"Where's your car?" he asked.

"In repair again."

He stopped. "How were you planning to get home?"

"Walk or take a cab." She shrugged. "What's the difference?"

"I don't like you out alone at night. It isn't safe." He opened the door of his sleek car and helped her in before walking to the driver's side. The darkness enveloped them, and she felt as if she had entered a cocoon of silence.

Inside the pizza parlor, the noise was deafening. A giant-screen television was showing a football game. On the far side of the room, a jukebox played. In a small cubicle, children and adults played video games. A loudspeaker blared the pizza orders.

Across a small table, Clint and Jordan grinned at each other.

"Very romantic place, Clint."

His eyes crinkled. "Speak up, Jordy. I can't hear a word you're saying."

It was wonderful, lighthearted fun. She was starving, and the first sip of beer seemed to go to her head. She and Clint managed to devour an entire pizza.

Afterward, with a wink, he said, "Come on, Jordy. I'll challenge you to a few video games. I happen to be very good. On the road, I can usually beat everyone in the band."

She laughed in delight. "You're on."

They played for over an hour. She beat him four out of five games.

"I think you've had a little experience at these things, lady."

"Little ole me?" She batted her eyelashes, grinning.

His hand pressed against the small of her back. "Come on. Let's get out of here. I hate losing to someone half my size."

Outside, a gentle rain fell, washing the city.

Jordan gave Clint directions to her small apartment. When they climbed the stairs, she fished in her pocket for the key, then placed it in his outstretched hand.

As he opened the door, she flipped on the light. Clint stared at the poster hanging over the table and flashed her a smile.

"Good-looking guy. Someone you know?"

She arched an eyebrow. "You think he's handsome? I always thought he was sort of funny looking. He's just someone I knew years ago. I hear he went off to the big city and made a name for himself."

The door closed softly behind him. He stared around the tiny apartment, noting the pile of papers on the table, the stack of books on the night table beside her bed. His gaze roamed over the brass bed, bright with colorful cushions tossed casually atop the crimson quilt.

A small love seat and chair in bright stripes added more color to the cheerful room. On a shelf he spotted a framed photograph of his family. Standing in the middle of the group, dwarfed by their size, was the tiny waif with the flowing hair and enormous eyes.

He tore his gaze from the picture, and studied the woman who had moved across the room.

"Would you like some coffee, Clint?"

He shook his head. "Don't bother, Jordy."

"A drink then?"

"No."

His look was direct, filled with all manner of unspoken meaning. Jordan felt a tiny jolt of fear course along her spine.

She turned her back, filling a kettle at the sink, just to keep busy.

He prowled the room, stopping for a moment to stare down at the bed.

"How are the songs for the new album coming, Clint?"

He picked up a small satin pillow, and traced one finger along the lace edging. "I seem to have developed a block." He dropped the pillow. "I can't think, can't get the words out."

"I guess the only thing to do is force yourself to keep working until you get beyond the block."

He glanced at her a moment, then walked to the shelf and picked up the family photo.

"Is that what you do—force yourself to keep working?" His back was to her. He seemed intent on the picture in his hands.

She spooned instant coffee into two cups, then stared at his back.

"Yes. But then, I'm not a songwriter." She ran her tongue over her lips. "But I've heard about writer's block. It seems to me that the only way to deal with it is to keep on working. Maybe you ought to go up to the farm for a while, and stick with it until you're satisfied."

He replaced the photo on the shelf, and looked across the room, studying the slight figure at the stove.

The kettle began whistling. As she lifted it, he turned to stare out the small window. Beneath the streetlight he could see the rain spattering onto black pavement. All along the darkened street, the lights wore halos in the misty rain. Her colorful apartment was the only bright spot in the darkness.

"Here." She set a cup of coffee on the end table. "You're so jumpy, Clint. Add a little more caffeine to those nerves."

He gave her a lopsided smile. "This stuff won't help. But it can't hurt either."

He stopped his pacing and sat down tensely on the edge of the sofa, sipping the steaming liquid.

His voice lowered. "The songs aren't good, Jordy. They're...hollow." He shrugged. "I can't put my finger on it. But they're not right. I don't feel the magic when I sing them."

"Is it the words or the melody?" She deliberately sat across the room, at the small table. It was better if there was a distance between them.

"The words. They're flat, meaningless." He stood abruptly, the restlessness in him driving him to movement.

"Clint."

He turned, and she saw the anguish in his eyes as he studied her. Without realizing it, her voice lowered to a breathless murmur.

"Why don't you go up to the farm until you've worked it all out?"

"I've tried that. Even the farm has lost its magic."

He paced again, aimlessly touching the books on her night table, picking up a paper, dropping it.

His stalking was making her edgy.

"I wish I had an answer for you, Clint." She stood. "But I'm a realist, a workhorse. You've always been the dreamer. I still think the best solution would be to get away from everything and work this out in solitude." Her voice warmed. "If anyone can write moving lyrics, it's you. You're the very best, you know."

He turned, a strange light in his eyes.

Avoiding him, she hurried to the stove. "More coffee?"

His voice took on a hard edge. "Why did you do it, Jordy?"

She looked up, startled at the abrupt question.

"Why did you wait until I was too far away to stop you, and then marry a stranger, someone you barely knew?"

When she was about fourteen years old, playing football with Clint and his brothers in the backyard, she had been hit with the ball smack in her stomach. The blow had stunned her, bringing her to her knees. All the wind had been knocked from her for a moment. It hurt to breathe too deeply. She had never forgotten that feeling. She had the same sensation now. Her breath felt lodged somewhere inside her, unable to get out.

She gripped the edge of the stove, steadying herself.

It wasn't writer's block. It wasn't the songs. All his prowling and tension had been over this. And now it was out in the open.

"My marriage to Marty is a closed subject." She was clenching her teeth so tightly they ached.

"I need to know. It's been eating away at me. I can't put it aside until we've talked about it."

She faced him across the room, seeing the hard set of his features, the dark, angry look in his eyes.

She shook her head slowly. "I can't, Clint. I won't talk about it. Especially to you."

He was across the room in quick strides, grasping her shoulders, nearly shaking her in his frustration.

"Pa isn't here now. It's just you and me." His voice took on a harsher edge. "One kiss. One damn kiss. I thought I was kissing a little kid on her sixteenth birthday. And I found a temptress in my arms, a woman in a child's body, exciting me in a way I'd only dreamed about." His dark gaze searched her face for answers. "I was willing to wait, Jordy. I thought the honorable thing was to give you time to grow up, to get the education Pa wanted you to have. I thought all little girls dreamed of high school proms and homecoming games and corsages.''

She stared into the dark pools of his eyes and saw the pain and anger there, completely exposed for the first time.

''But you couldn't wait, could you, Jordy? While I was off in the service, you grew up hard-and-fast.'' He shook his head, as if still disbelieving. ''When I got the letter from Glen, I couldn't believe it. All he wrote was, 'Little Jordy ran off and married a fast-talking salesman.' ''

''You make it sound so...'' She lowered her head. ''Let me go, Clint.''

He released her as if the touch of her repelled him. ''That's the problem, Jordy,'' he said in a whisper. ''I keep trying to let you go.'' His voice rose. ''Give me a good reason for your marriage to Marty.''

''I have no intention of discussing him. He's dead, Clint. Leave it be.''

He swept his hand to indicate the entire room. ''There's not one thing here to show you were ever married to him. Not one picture. Nothing of his. Why?''

Her control snapped. Anger deepened her voice. ''I said drop it, Clint. I have no intention of discussing this anymore. It's a closed chapter in my life. Now I want you to leave.''

As she turned away, his arms came around her waist. Shocked, she stiffened, feeling him in every nerve ending of her body. He turned her, ever so slowly, in his arms, until she was facing him.

"Jordy." The name seemed wrenched from him.

Panic constricted her throat. "Please don't, Clint."

His hands moved up to cup her face. His voice was a raw whisper. "I have to, Jordy. I've wanted to do this since you first walked back into my life."

"No..."

As his face descended, he saw the flutter of her dark eyelashes. For one brief instant, her eyes widened. Then the lashes lowered. Her eyes closed.

His lips found hers, for one exquisite moment, soft, hesitant. The kiss was as gentle as a whisper, tasting, without asking more. Yet her senses sharpened and she was exquisitely aware of his body just a heartbeat away.

As he pressed his mouth to hers, he felt her stiffen. Her heart hammered wildly in her chest. His tongue feathered lightly over hers. Then the kiss came alive, hot, searing, as his hands dropped to her shoulders, drawing her closer.

Her hands gripped his waist. She felt as if the world was spinning dangerously out of control. All the nights she had dreamed of this, all the years she had waited, exploded into the reality of this kiss. Heat coursed through her veins, and she clung to him as if her life depended on it.

His hands moved down her back, molding her tightly to his length, and all the while his mouth continued to move over hers, drawing her further into desire. Her flesh was warm where his hands seemed to burn through the soft fabric of her blouse.

Her hands encircled his neck as she stood taller, needing to reach up to him, wanting to feel every part of him touching her.

"My God, Jordy, how I missed you." His lips pressed into a tangle of hair and he drew her so close she could feel his erratic heartbeat through her shirt.

His lips burned a trail of fire along her temple and cheek, then once again claimed her mouth. She was helpless to stop him. It felt so good to be held in his arms.

He drank of her, draining her, and in turn she took from him the strength, the passion surging through him. His hands inched along her sides, until they found the soft swell of breasts beneath her shirt. His thumbs traced their roundness, felt them straining tautly against the thin barrier.

She heard a little moan, and realized it was her own voice, sounding strangely distant and strangled in her throat.

"Please, Clint. You have to stop." Her lips moved against his mouth, so that the words seemed swallowed by him. Had she spoken, or dreamed it?

He paused, lifting his head to study her face. In the light spilling over her face, he could see her eyes, wide and shimmering with unshed tears.

It had only been a kiss. Nothing more. And yet he had taken more of her in that simple gesture than if she had given him her body. She was stunned at the depth of passion that had flowed between them.

Reaching out a fingertip to brush away a tear, he pulled her gently into his embrace.

"Jordy, please don't cry. I don't ever want to make you cry."

He held her as if she were a fragile china doll, rocking her ever so gently, like a child.

"I'm sorry, Jordy. I had no right." His lips were warm where they pressed against her temple, murmuring words of endearment.

He felt her stiffen. "You don't need to worry, Clint." Her voice was muffled against his chest. "I'm not crying." She pushed herself a little away from him and met his eyes. "I never cry."

Lifting her chin with his hand, he stared down at her stricken face. With a tender smile, he murmured, "Of course you don't. I just forgot that for a minute." The roguish smile grew. "Always the tough little cookie, weren't you?"

She took in a deep breath, controlling the shudder that threatened. "That's right. Now Clint, you'd better go."

"Let me stay the night."

"No." The single word was harsh, bitter.

"You don't mean that. I know what you felt just now. I felt it too. There's no denying that you're a woman, with a woman's needs. You're not that little sixteen-year-old anymore. Let me stay, Jordy. I need you."

She pushed free and took a step back, avoiding his touch. "You don't understand, Clint. You're right about one thing. I'm definitely not that little girl anymore. And that's all the more reason why you're not staying. I won't get conned again. I learned from an expert. If I'm ever foolish enough to fall in love again, it will be on my terms.''

He studied the tight line of her mouth, her heaving shoulders as she sought to control herself. But was it passion she sought to control, or anger?

''Your terms?'' He studied her. ''And what are your terms, Jordy?''

''I control my life now, Clint. No one makes my decisions for me. I'll love whom I please, when I please. But it will be my decision.''

Pain. He saw it in her eyes. Sharp, fleeting. Then she quickly composed herself. How deeply had she been hurt? He cursed his clumsiness. He had no right to inflict more pain on her.

''I'm . . . sorry.'' Clint spoke the words softly, as a defense against the self-loathing he felt at the realization that he had hurt her.

She turned away, forcing a casual tone she didn't feel. ''Good night, Clint. Thanks for the pizza.''

For long moments he paused, contemplating his next move. He thought about all the convincing arguments he could give her. He didn't want to go yet. He would use any excuse to stay. But the time wasn't right now. The moment had passed.

Control. She said she needed to control her life. And why not? From her earliest days, people had been making decisions that would affect her future. She had earned the right to be master of her own fate.

He gave one last glance at her rigid back, then opened the door in defeat.

''Sleep well, Jordy.''

When the door closed, she locked it. For long moments she leaned weakly against it, feeling the pounding of her heartbeat. Had Clint guessed how close she had come to giving in to him? She shook her head, as if to dispel any lingering thoughts of him, then moved mechanically about the room, picking up the coffee cups, rinsing them. When there was nothing left to occupy her time, she undressed, crawled between the covers and rolled to her stomach. With her hands balled into fists, she pressed her face into the pillow.

There was nothing to cry about. He had never been hers. She had lost nothing.

Some dreams die of natural causes, or are shoved aside by better ones. And some struggle for life against incredible odds. They take fragile root between layers of harsh rock, thrive instead of withering away, only to be shattered beneath the heavy load of reality.

Oh, God, she was no good at this. Clint was going to crowd her thoughts again. Awake or asleep, he would be there, distracting her. Why couldn't she have left the dreaming to an expert!

Chapter Four

By morning the rain had stopped. The streets glistened with a freshly washed appearance. Jordan peered from her apartment window, grateful for the sunshine. Feeling jumpy and irritable, she welcomed all the help she could get to improve the day.

Adding a touch of lightener beneath her eyes to hide the dark circles, she ran a brush through the tangles, then with a shake of her head, gave up in despair. This was one of those days when her hair seemed to have a mind of its own.

The band was rehearsing today. Clint wanted them to begin preparing the first three of the songs they would record on the album.

Jordan spent a hectic day at the office, sorting and responding to her mail and returning the dozens of messages left on the answering machine. She felt a twinge of regret every time she had to refuse another publicity appearance on Clint's behalf. Some of them were a publicity agent's dream. But she knew that Clint's instincts were correct. He really needed this time before the recording session to withdraw a little from the public eye.

She made a face at the bitter, lukewarm coffee in her pot and dumped the day-old contents down the drain. As she returned to her desk, Jordan continued to sort through the mail while she absently picked up the phone.

"J.D? I think you'd better get over here."

Frankie Tanner's voice was an octave higher than usual. Frankie was the band's road manager. Although only nineteen, he had proven himself adept at collecting his share of the adoring young girls who were eager to know anyone connected with Clint Donner.

"What's wrong, Frankie?" Jordan swiveled her chair to glance out the smudged office window, and was jolted to note that it was already growing dark. Where had the day gone?

She could hear him taking several deep breaths before starting. He must have run all the way to the phone.

"Clint's been real edgy all day. And he's been jumping all over Randy every time he misses a beat." His voice lowered suddenly, and Jordan realized someone must have walked close enough to overhear his side of the conversation. "J.D., you seem to handle Clint's moods better than anyone. I think you'd better get over here before this thing ends in a real knockdown brawl."

"I'm on my way."

In her eagerness to replace the receiver, she knocked over a neat pile of correspondence, and watched in dismay as papers drifted and scattered about the floor. Snatching her purse from the desk drawer, she hurried out and locked the door. Tomorrow she would deal with the mail.

The rehearsal hall was a square building with no windows. The cement block structure had been painted mud brown. Situated on a side street in an area of Nashville called Music Row, it gave no indication on the outside of what went on inside.

Jordan pushed open the heavy door, expecting to hear the sound of music. Instead, she heard the discordant sound of voices raised in anger.

"Where's your brain today, Randy? Weren't you listening? I just told you. I want this chord to build slowly here, then swell, then fade."

Clint had his back to her as he directed those angry words at his drummer. Surrounded by the other musicians, they faced each other like boxers in a ring.

"And I say you're wrong, Clint. You're trying for drama, but all you're doing is slowing the beat. It's choppy. It's..." Still holding the drumsticks, he threw up his hands in a gesture of despair. "It's all wrong. The whole thing is flat."

"I see. Now you've decided to rewrite my music, is that it, Randy?"

Jordan saw Randy blanch before he turned away quickly.

The others watched in strained silence, powerless to interrupt what the two men were saying to each other.

Jordan knew their friendship had weathered many storms. Randy and Clint had started out together. Two farm boys with a dream of creating music. They had gone through the service together, taken college courses together, and in their spare time, had studied and practiced and worked to become musicians. It would take more than a few hateful words to destroy the strong bond between them. Still . . .

Jordan had never seen Clint so careless of another's feelings. She knew him to be sensitive and caring. The depth of his frustration worried her.

She stepped from the shadows. "How about a dinner break?"

At the sound of her voice, Clint's head came up sharply.

Frankie hurried across the room. "Hey, J.D. I'm glad to see you." Relief warmed his voice. "I can take everybody's order and pick something up."

Jordan gave him a gentle smile. His lingering anxiety was evident in his troubled gray eyes.

"I think it might be better if we all went out somewhere. Clint, how about that romantic pizza joint you took me to the other night?"

Her humor didn't stir him. Clint studied her silently, without expression. Then he shrugged.

"Okay. I guess we could all use a break. Why don't you take everybody out, and get them back here by eight o'clock."

"You need dinner too, Clint."

"No. I want to go over a few things."

She studied his stiff posture, then tossed her car keys to their road manager. "Here, Frankie. You take care of it."

One by one, the musicians followed him out, relieved at the break. As Randy hesitated, Clint dropped his hand on his drummer's shoulder.

"Randy, I'm sorry. You shouldn't have to take the heat when I'm like this."

His friend met his direct gaze, then nodded. "Yeah. I know, Clint. It's okay. We'll work it out."

Before walking out the door, Randy gave Jordan a sardonic smile. "Careful, J.D. You could be next."

At the door he stopped, and with his hand on the knob, turned. "Would you explain to this bundle of nerves that it isn't the end of the world?"

She shot him a grateful smile, and waited in silence until the door closed behind him.

"He's right, you know."

Clint expelled an angry breath and walked away from her. Bent over his music, he began to make notes. For long moments, she watched without interrupting.

She moved closer. "You can't keep this up, Clint. Pretty soon, the whole band will be sniping at each other."

He threw down the pages of music he was holding, sending a pencil flying.

"Is that all you came here to say, Jordy? If so, you've had your say. Now why don't you leave and let me get on with my work."

The temper she held in such tight control began to get the better of her.

"Oh, stop being so dramatic, Clint. Did it ever occur to you that you're not the only one here with a job to do? I know it isn't always easy, but you just have to get rid of whatever frustrations are bothering you and get on with it."

He ran a hand through his hair, then pinned her with his dark gaze.

"Thank you for those pearls of wisdom. Is that how you run your life, Jordy? Just get rid of the frustrations?"

She started to turn away, but his hand caught her, holding her back.

He drew her closer. His voice was a low growl. "Maybe you'd like to help me get rid of my frustrations." His lips grazed her temple.

"Don't, Clint."

"Don't? You mean you don't like it when I touch you like this?"

She shrank back, avoiding him.

"You don't like it when I hold you?" His hands gripped her shoulders, drawing her close against him.

Instinctively, she brought her hands to his chest to stop him.

"Don't push away from me, Jordy." His words, breathed against her temple, sent a shaft of heat along her spine. "Don't pretend you don't want this."

Her eyes widened as his head bent to her. For a moment, she saw his narrowed look of fury. Then his lips covered hers.

The kiss was heated with anger. The hands that gripped her shoulders were without tenderness. She kept her fists between them, an impotent barrier.

But in the instant their lips touched, she felt the anger within him dissolving. He changed the angle of his kiss, tasting, nibbling. The hands that clutched her shoulders now moved gently to the small of her back, drawing her even closer. He felt her gradually relax against him; her hands slid around his waist.

He lifted his face to study her. His lips brushed her forehead, her eyelids, then trailed slowly across her cheek, before again finding her mouth.

The kiss was seductive, practiced, then grew more urgent as he felt her willing response.

Against her will, Jordan was losing herself. She could feel herself slipping away, drifting, giving up her control to the only man who would ever have this power over her.

He murmured against her throat, and felt the little shiver that passed through her. She arched herself in his arms, loving the feel of his lips on her skin. He brought his lips lower. As he grazed her breast, he heard a soft moan that might have been protest or desire. When he lifted his lips to hers, he found them parted in invitation. The kiss grew hotter, as he felt her need beginning to match his.

His arms encircled her, drawing her so tightly to him they felt like one. His mouth was plundering hers now, feeding on the need she could no longer hide.

How long had it been since she had felt like this? So long. A lifetime of needing to feel Clint's embrace. Their bodies were heated now. There was no room for thought. There was only Clint, and her burning ache for him.

"Jordy. Oh God, Jordy. I need you." His words were spoken inside her mouth, against her ear, along her throat. "I need you, Jordy. Now. Let me love you."

Passion clouded her thinking. His lips and hands roamed at will, taking her too far to resist. She wanted the same release he was seeking. She needed him.

His lips moved over hers, seeming to take the very breath from her lungs. She slid her hands along his chest, then encircled his neck. For long moments, she cradled his head in her hands, knowing that she was losing herself to this man, yet wanting the pleasure his touch brought.

With a last burst of sanity, she found the strength to push him away. "No. No more, Clint."

For one shocked instant, he froze. She forced air into her lungs, taking deep breaths.

"You don't mean that." He caught her by the shoulders, determined to draw her closer.

She shook her head. "I said no."

"Why, Jordy?" His voice lowered dangerously. "You know you wanted this as much as I."

"It was a mistake."

"Was it?" He was angry now. "Just what kind of game are you playing with me, Jordy? Are you still that little temptress, taking me higher than I've ever been before, then dropping me just for the pleasure of it?" His eyes glittered. "Is this some kind of an ego thing with you? Do you just want to see me squirm?"

She turned away, pressing her hands to flaming cheeks, shaking her head against his cruel words. "I didn't start this, Clint. I only came here to keep you from fighting with your band. I didn't want . . .''

"You wanted, all right. You wanted it as badly as I did. You still do."

"I told you. I'll love on my terms." She turned back, meeting his look boldly. "Ours is a professional relationship only. Now if you'd like to find a manager who's willing to cater to your personal needs . . ."

"That won't be necessary." For what seemed an eternity, he studied her. Then he turned his back on her and stalked back to his music. Bending, he picked up the pencil. "There are plenty of women available for that."

She flinched as if he had slapped her. Without another glance in her direction, he began to concentrate on his work.

She was stung by his coldness. Was it just a defense against her rejection? Or was she so unimportant that he could turn his feelings on and off at will?

For long moments she stood watching him. He had completely tuned her out. He was the professional now, back in control, interested only in his work.

When the door closed softly behind Jordan, he didn't even bother to look up.

Jordan stood outside the rehearsal hall, shivering in the evening chill, until the band returned with her car. Refreshed now, they emerged laughing and chatting, eager for another session. They would rehearse until the early hours of the morning.

"J.D." Randy caught her arm and glanced at her tight features, which were illuminated beneath the streetlight. "Everything okay?"

"Sure, Randy. Everything's fine." She lowered her head, avoiding his gaze.

"Clint's got a lot on his mind right now." The drummer patted her arm affectionately. "You and I know him well enough to understand that he doesn't mean half of what he says."

She nodded, not trusting her voice. Then she offered him a bleak smile before climbing behind the wheel of her battered old car.

While the rest of the band disappeared inside the hall, Randy stood alone, watching the taillights move slowly down the street before the car merged into traffic.

The clock showed four in the morning. Inside the windowless hall, it could have been day or night. The hours blended together into a timeless blur of sound.

Billy Peters, hunching over the keys of the piano, flexed his tired fingers. Over six feet tall, bone thin, his myopic eyes framed by wire-rimmed glasses, Billy appeared to be all elbows and knees. He had earned the nickname Spiderman.

"I want to try that last number again," Clint said. "From the beginning."

Billy moaned, and Clint shot him a dark look.

As the band started, Billy was a beat late, but managed to catch up.

Clint exploded, swearing loudly. A sudden quiet echoed through the hall. The musicians looked up expectantly.

"Wake up, Spider. We're not going home until we get this right."

"The hell we're not!" Billy slammed down the cover on the piano and shoved back the stool.

"Sit down, Spider." Clint started toward the piano, fists clenched at his sides. "I said we're going to keep going."

"And I say you can finish this rehearsal without me. In fact, maybe you'd better start looking for another piano man, Clint. I've got a wife at home I'd like to see once in a while."

"We'd all like to get home. But the music isn't right yet."

"Listen, pal." Billy faced Clint, thin arms protruding incongruously from the sleeves of his T-shirt. "The way you've been acting lately, I don't think you have a home to go to. Who'd have you? You probably have to crawl under a rock somewhere."

They faced each other for a lingering moment, then Billy swung away. A moment later, they heard the slamming of the door.

In the silence that followed, Randy tapped his drumsticks distractedly, then stood and slowly made his way to Clint's side. In a voice barely above a whisper, he said, "I think we've all had it tonight, Clint. Let's call it quits."

Clint met his friend's gaze, then nodded and picked up his music.

Seeing his distress, Randy smoothly took charge. "We'll see everybody tomorrow afternoon. How about three o'clock?" He glanced at Clint, who nodded again.

Randy turned back to the others. "Right. Three. Good night." With a slight smile he added, "Or should I say good morning?"

With hushed comments, the band members made their way from the hall. Their complete exhaustion was evident on their strained features.

When they were alone, Randy carefully covered his drums, then perched on a stool, watching Clint make notes on his music.

"What's really eating at you, Clint?" The voice was a low, easy drawl.

"This album is important—to all of us. You know that, Randy." Clint continued to stare at the music, avoiding his friend's eyes.

"We've recorded albums before. All of them were important. But I've never seen you take out your tensions on the guys in the band before." His voice lowered. "It's something else, Clint. I think we both know what it is."

Clint looked up from the music to meet his friend's level gaze.

"She's something special, you know. I think it's time to tell the lady how you feel." Randy's fingers, usually tapping out a rhythm on anything available, had gone very still.

Clint rubbed his hand across his forehead. "You always could read me." His gaze lowered to the floor.

"I've tried. She's having none of it." Clint's voice was clipped.

"I see." Randy studied his friend with new understanding. "Are you sure you've been straight with her? Maybe she thinks you're just—" he shrugged, searching for a phrase "—playing with her. Maybe if you tried again..."

Clint stood, signaling an end to the conversation. "Don't worry about it, Randy. I'll work it out." He took a deep breath, then released it slowly. "Look, would you mind working with the band alone for a while? You know how I want these numbers to go."

Randy nodded. "No problem. What about you?"

Clint caught up all the loose sheets of music and stuffed them into a briefcase. "I'm not doing anyone any good around here. All I've managed to accomplish in the last few days is to alienate most of my friends."

He walked to the door, then turned with a haunted look. "I don't know if it will do any good, but I think I'll run up to the farm for a while. Maybe I can work myself out of this slump."

Clint set the suitcase on the floor, then walked to the window, staring at the black-robed night. The flame of his lighter flared for a moment, igniting the tip of a cigarette. This marked the ending of his tenth attempt to quit smoking.

He drew deeply on the cigarette, filling his lungs. Why had he let Jordy back into his life? He was reaching a crossroads in his career. He knew it. All the dues had been paid. It was time for stardom. The whole group sensed it. And now, instead of enjoying it, savoring the triumph, he was letting her get in the way of his satisfaction.

He leaned a hip against the windowsill, watching the distant lights of a plane. In the beginning, it had been the glamor, the applause, the crowds. And the music. Always the music.

When the money came in, he convinced himself that he could do wonderful things for his family. And he had. Glen had the biggest law firm in Knoxville. And if he chose to go into the political arena, he'd need plenty of financial backers. Earl's farm was the pride of Overton County. And Danny. Clint smiled in the darkness, just thinking of his oldest brother. Danny had always been the one who brought home the wounded birds, the strays. People and animals sensed Danny's gentleness. He was meant to be a country doctor. And he might not have made it through medical school without Clint's help.

But now? Clint drew deeply on the cigarette and prowled the room. All this time, he had convinced himself that the music and the applause and his loving family would be enough. Success had been easy to take. But Jordy's presence changed everything.

She was there, like an ache, reminding him of the one thing he had wanted more than the fame, more than life itself.

Glen had been aware of it, years ago. All of them, with the exception of the innocent Jordy, had recognized his feelings. With the cool logic of a budding lawyer, Glen had advised him to get her out of his system.

"Take my advice, Clint. If you ever get the chance, love her all through the night. You'll soon see there's no magic there. It's just that old devil—unrequited love."

Angrily, Clint stubbed out the cigarette. Would that have cured him? If he had had her, just once, would he be over her for good?

Swearing, he paced the room, feeling the anger and frustration building inside him. Why had he allowed her to become his manager? Why had he set himself up for this? Why did he let her get under his skin time and again? He wanted her. He woke up wanting her, and fell asleep wanting her. Thinking about her was driving him crazy.

He needed to move, to keep busy. It was the only way to blot her from his mind.

With quick jerking motions, he pulled on a jacket and picked up the suitcase. For the next two hours he could speed along the deserted highways toward the farm, and hope that the music would crowd out all other thoughts.

He paused at the door, and set down the luggage. It was no good. His anger was no justification for the way he had hurt her tonight. He had seen the pain his words had inflicted. And she'd been hurt too many times in the past.

Without taking time to consider what he was doing, he dialed her number. A glance at the clock on the nightstand told him it was four-thirty.

The sound of the telephone ringing on the other end of the line furrowed his brow. He ought to hang up and let her sleep. Before he had time to reconsider, the phone was answered.

"Hello?" Her voice was soft and muffled from sleep.

"Jordy."

At his familiar voice, tiny tremors rippled through her.

"I'm sorry to wake you like this." He slumped down on the edge of the bed.

"Clint." She leaned on her elbow, struggling to clear her sleep-fogged brain. "What's wrong?"

"Nothing. Everything. I feel really lousy. I had no right to say or do those things tonight. I had to call and tell you how sorry I am."

"Oh." She leaned back, suddenly relieved that it wasn't another crisis.

"I had no right to take out my anxieties on you tonight, Jordy."

She was silent for long moments, and he feared she would hang up on him.

"It's all right, Clint. I understand the pressures of the business. This album means everything to you."

"No." He took a deep breath. "It isn't the album. It isn't the pressures of the business." After a long pause, he said softly, "I had no right to force myself on you, Jordy. It won't happen again. I don't know what you've been through these past years. I only know you deserve better treatment than I've been giving you. I promise you, you won't have to fight me ever again."

He heard the soft sigh before she spoke. "Thank you, Clint."

The tension began to drain from him.

She paused. "Clint?"

"Yes?"

"What time is it?"

"Four-thirty." He plumped the pillow and leaned back, wondering what she wore to bed. He loved hearing her sleepy voice. "Go back to sleep now, Jordy. I'll see you in a few days or so."

She struggled to sit up. "A few days! Where are you going?"

"To the farm. I need to get away." He chuckled, and the warmth of the sound washed over her. "As I recall, my manager advised me to find a way to work out my frustrations and then get on with it. Very sound advice."

She felt the sudden sting of disappointment. He was going away.

"Jordy, sleep late if you want. There's no need to rush in to work. In fact, take a few days off. You've been working too hard. You've earned a little vacation."

She laughed, a deliciously warm sound that melted the last of the tension from him. "Don't be silly. I can always find lots of work to do."

"I know. You're the hardest worker I've ever met. Go back to sleep now, Jordy."

She could hear the change in his voice. At first, it had been edged with tension, or anger, or both. Now the deep drawl was softer, easier.

"Good night, Clint."

His hand rested for long moments on the phone. Then he rose, strode purposefully across the room and picked up his luggage.

The drive would be peaceful now. Jordy would still be in his thoughts, but the thoughts would no longer be tormented. They would be tranquil now; they wouldn't crowd out the music. In fact, she would be the music.

Chapter Five

"Ouch!"

Jordan grimaced as the rubber band broke, snapping against her finger.

Holding the clump of hair in one hand, she rummaged through drawers with the other until she found a new rubber band. She barely glanced in the mirror at the two clusters of hair that streamed down past each shoulder. There was no need to fuss about her appearance today. No need to bother about makeup. She was dressed in narrow jeans and a plaid shirt. She padded across the room and felt under her bed for her faded sneakers.

Jordan had decided to spend the day cleaning out the files. It was the perfect opportunity, while Clint was away.

On her way to work she picked up a container of coffee and an egg and sausage wrapped in a hamburger bun. After two bites and two sips, both grew cold on the desk.

By late morning, the desk and floor were littered with file folders as she sorted and discarded unnecessary correspondence, old issues of trade papers and magazines. The wastebasket was overflowing with paper.

When the phone rang, she had to sift through the mountain of mail on her desk just to find it.

"Yes. Hello. Clint Donner Enterprises." Jordan pushed a wayward strand of hair behind her ear and felt the rubber band break.

"Mr. Donner, please." The woman's voice was clipped, professional.

"I'm sorry. Mr. Donner is unavailable. May I take a message?"

The woman sighed. "Mr. Donner phoned this morning to confirm that he'd be performing here around two o'clock. I just realized that he might need some additional outlets or extension cords. Would you be able to advise me?"

Jordan straightened. "You must be mistaken. Mr. Donner is out of town for a couple of days. He's preparing for a recording session. He isn't doing any public appearances."

After a slight pause, the woman said, "I only know that Mr. Donner phoned me this morning and said he'd be stopping by at two o'clock. He's done this sort of thing before, but our custodian, Mr. Bell, always saw to the details. Mr. Bell is home sick today, and I just wanted to be prepared in case he needed any-thing."

Jordan hurried around her desk, banged her knee on the overflowing wastebasket, and pulled out a pen and notepad. "If you'll give me your name, address and phone number, I'll try to reach Mr. Donner and get back to you."

"I'm Mrs. Post at the Roper School in Anderson-ville."

Jordan scribbled the phone number and hung up the phone, then hurriedly dialed Clint's number at the farm. There was no answer.

She glanced at her watch. If she left now, she'd be in Andersonville by two o'clock. Curiosity was eating at her. She had to know why Clint would volunteer to entertain school children at a time like this.

She stared around the office. Litter covered every inch of space. She gave a sigh of regret. It wasn't something she'd look forward to in the morning. But it couldn't be helped.

Tugging loose the other rubber band, she ran a brush through the wild tangles, added some gloss to her lips and hurried out the door.

By the time Jordan parked her car at the Roper School, her nerves were frazzled. She had made two wrong turns. The second one took her at least thirty miles out of her way. She had stopped for directions, only to be given conflicting ones by the two men at the gas station. Finally, relying on a road map given her by a sympathetic attendant, she had found her desti-nation. She recognized Clint's car, and gave a sigh of relief.

Half running, she entered the one story building and stopped at the office. A young secretary looked up smiling.

"Hello. Can I help you?"

With one hand, Jordan flicked her hair back and returned the smile. "I'm looking for Clint Donner. I understand he's performing here today."

The smile widened. "Oh yes. Isn't he wonderful! He's down the hall, in the auditorium. As soon as my replacement comes, I'll be going there too. Here, let me show you the way."

With a whirr of machinery, the young woman rounded the corner of the desk. Jordan stared at the electric wheelchair, then back at the girl's face.

In the doorway, she pointed and said brightly, "Just follow this hallway to the end, then turn left. There are orange and yellow arrows showing the way."

"Thank you."

The long, confusing drive, the snarled traffic, her cranky old car, were all forgotten. Jordan could see only the beautiful smile on the young woman's face.

She was more subdued as she approached the auditorium. Beyond, Jordan heard Clint's voice, singing a childhood refrain. She eased through the doorway, and stopped.

He was strumming an old guitar. She recognized it as one of the first ones he had ever bought, with money saved by working after school. It had been his constant companion in college, and he had even hauled it along when he went into the service.

All the children's voices joined in the chorus, and Jordan stared around the room in amazement. She realized with a jolt that every child in the room was either in a wheelchair, on crutches or needed special help of some sort. She hadn't realized until this moment that this was a school for the handicapped.

As he strummed his guitar and moved through the crowd, Clint glanced up and saw her in the doorway. Surprise, then pleasure, showed in his eyes. He continued leading the children in song, as he made his way to her side.

While the children sang the chorus, he paused.

"Hello, Jordy. Mrs. Post told me she phoned you. But I didn't expect you to drive all this way."

Jordan was so glad to see him, she didn't know if she could trust her voice. "I didn't mind the drive. I had to satisfy my curiosity. Besides," she reminded him dryly, "I am your manager. I'm supposed to know about every appearance in advance."

"Sorry about that. I should have let you in on this. But I just decided on the spur of the moment. It's something I needed to do for myself."

She looked wonderful. On anyone else, he realized, those clothes would have looked ordinary. On another woman, that hair would look all wrong. But she was Jordy. She was unique. He wanted to kiss the two bright spots of color on her cheeks. Instead, he lifted a hand. "Come on inside, and make yourself comfortable."

She reached up to touch his chin. "I see something new's been added. Have you decided to change your image and grow a beard, or are you just tired of shaving?"

"Up at the farm there aren't too many people to see me. I thought I'd take a vacation from shaving. Like it?"

She would think he was the handsomest man in the world even if he shaved his head. She shrugged. "If you go for the caveman look, I suppose it's okay."

She followed him in and found a place beside a little blond girl in a wheelchair.

"We have a guest today," Clint told the children. "Maybe if you coax her, you can get my manager, Jordan Hunter, to sing for you."

Her eyes went wide. She shot him a murderous look.

As the children urged, she shook her head. "You don't understand. I can't even carry a tune. After a couple of notes, you'll all be begging me to stop."

The crowd wouldn't be satisfied. They giggled, whistled and stomped, until, to quiet them, Jordan stood.

"Okay, you'll be sorry."

While Clint strummed his guitar, and grinned at her like a conspirator, Jordan sang a silly song Clint and his brothers had taught her. The words made no sense, except to the young, or the young at heart. Luckily, the children knew the words and chimed in, allowing her to hiss under her breath, "I'll get you for this, Clint Donner."

"You have to watch out for cavemen. We have no scruples." He winked at her, and her heart did a somersault.

On the second chorus, she invited Clint to sing the harmony. With the children clapping, he couldn't refuse. As he bent closer, she deliberately sang off-key, and nearly choked on her laughter as she saw him wince at the grating sound.

At her deadpan performance, he told the audience, "I don't think we'll ask Ms. Hunter to do an encore."

She bowed primly, but he saw the glint of humor that lit her eyes.

After her performance, Jordan was invited to sit in the circle of students, completely accepted as one of them. She relaxed, and found herself as caught up in the magic of Clint's charm as the children.

He played and sang for nearly two hours. Some pieces were his own songs, and Jordan realized that the children knew all the words. Others were children's songs, silly or bouncy, that brought giggles to his audience.

Occasionally his gaze would wander over the crowd, seeking out the beautiful woman surrounded by the happy faces of children. When he first glanced, she was holding a little girl's hand. The next time he saw her, she and the frail dark-skinned boy in her lap were keeping time to the music. He watched as smaller children came up to hug her, to stroke her silken hair, or just to share a smile. The children seemed to know instinctively that they could be at ease with her.

While Clint entertained them, Jordan watched the reaction of the children and teachers alike. They adored him. He gave as much of himself to them as he did to the throngs of people who were willing to pay any amount to fill stadiums or orchestra halls to watch him perform.

He made easy conversation with them, told silly jokes, asked them questions. And as often as they called out a favorite song, he obliged by performing it.

Mopping his forehead, Clint announced that he would do only one last song. The crowd moaned. He chuckled, and held up his hand.

"Didn't I time this so you wouldn't have any more classes this afternoon?"

The children shrieked their appreciation.

"Now, don't you think we all deserve to get out of here in time for dinner?"

Again the children laughed and applauded.

"All right. So this has to be my last song. I'd like to sing you a song my grandfather taught me."

He began to sing a lullaby. The room was hushed as the audience lost themselves in the poignant song. Suddenly, a clear child's voice joined Clint's. Jordan strained to see who possessed such a marvelous voice. She turned to see a little boy of eight or nine. He was seated in a wheelchair, his thin legs showing years of disuse. Then she saw his face. Fine blond hair surrounded pale, almost iridescent skin. He had the face of an angel. His gaze was locked on Clint, a look of pure love lighting his blue eyes. When the song ended, there was a moment of silence. Then the crowd of children in the auditorium erupted into applause.

Clint crossed the room to kneel beside the boy's wheelchair.

"That was beautiful. Thank you for helping me. What's your name?"

"Stevie." The high-pitched voice, which had never wavered during the song, now trembled.

"Do you play, Stevie?" Clint asked the boy as he lifted the cord from around his own neck and placed it around the boy's.

"No. I can't make my fingers stay on the strings."

"I know. It's hard, even for me." Clint adjusted the guitar on the boy's lap and positioned his fingers over the child's.

He strummed the boy's fingers across the strings, and the children whistled and stomped. Stevie stared adoringly at Clint's face.

"My fingers won't stay there, see?"

He held a frail, trembling hand aloft.

Clint smiled. "You can do it. Watch." Again he positioned the fingers, and this time he let Stevie strum the chord himself.

Again the crowd cheered.

"I'll tell you what, Stevie. Why don't you keep this old guitar for me? While I'm gone, you can practice on it. And whenever I get a chance to stop by, you can be my accompanist."

"You mean it?" The blue eyes were shining.

"Yes. I know you'll take good care of it. And you'll practice faithfully?"

"I sure will, Clint."

"Good. It means a lot to me to know that you'll take good care of this old friend." Clint lovingly patted the guitar, then solemnly shook Stevie's hand.

Jordan swallowed down the lump that had formed in her throat.

Several of the children rolled their wheelchairs near Stevie's to examine his new treasure and to share in the excitement of his sudden celebrity status. He was beaming.

As the teachers began moving the children slowly from the auditorium, Clint picked up a little girl on crutches and carried her while pushing an older boy in a wheelchair. Jordan watched as ambulatory students assisted others in need. Everyone was smiling, laughing, still caught up in the excitement generated by Clint's presence.

She pushed a young girl in a wheelchair through the wide doors and down the hall. At the entrance, Jordan stopped to say goodbye. The girl reached up and hugged her.

With a last smile at the children, Clint caught Jordan's hand and they both strolled from the school. The sound of applause and shouted goodbyes could still be heard as they walked down the long ramp and out to their parked cars.

Their hands were still linked.

"Do you do this often, Mr. Donner?"

He stared down at their hands.

"Not as often as I'd like."

"How did you happen to find these kids?" She studied his bowed head.

He looked up, and she felt the familiar jolt as his gaze met hers. "My brother Danny told me about them. He gives them as much free medical help as he can."

She nodded. That was what she'd expect from Danny.

"It was a wonderful treat for them."

"I can't think of a better tonic for me than these kids." His voice had grown deeper. "They give me more than I could ever give them."

She wondered if the love she felt for him at this moment was obvious. "You were wonderful, Clint."

He grinned, and she felt a rush of heat. "Thanks, Jordy. You were great too. I may start taking you along for a backup." He brushed a strand of hair from her cheek. "Provided you promise not to purposely sing off-key again."

She reached up and stroked the dark beard that had begun to cover his chin. "And I may even learn to like looking at a fierce caveman. How are you getting along with your new songs? Think you'll be back by tomorrow?"

He dropped her hand. She felt instantly chilled.

"No. I'll need more time."

More time. She felt a sudden ache. Standing this close to him, she realized how tired he looked. She fought down a yearning to wrap her arms about him and offer him warmth and rest and—more.

In the fading light, her wild tumble of dark hair gleamed blue-black. The green eyes staring at him glowed like a cat's.

He fought down a sudden, shocking surge of desire. He wanted to crush her to him, to feel her slender body tremble at his touch. He wanted to kiss her, stroke her, until she felt for him what he felt for her. The need for her was becoming some sort of savage fury. The thought of her distracted him from his work. And he couldn't even escape her in dreams. At night, she crept into his sleep, until he found himself pacing the floor, seeking a release.

But he had made her a promise. She would never have to fight him again. It was important for her to control her own destiny. He had no right to put his needs before hers.

"Will you go back to the farm now, Clint?"

"Uh hum. And you? Going back to the city?"

She nodded, feeling close to tears. She wanted him to take her in his arms. She wanted him to beg her to stay with him.

He opened her car door. She hesitated for a moment, then reluctantly climbed in. He leaned down, and for a second she thought he would kiss her.

He inhaled her perfume. His fist clenched at his side. "Drive carefully, Jordy."

He closed the door, and she started the ignition.

The sun had gone down. Maybe it had gone out completely. She knew it had gone out of her life.

Chapter Six

"Hi, Randy. How's it going?"

Warm hazel eyes regarded her for a moment before crinkling into a smile.

"Fine, J.D." He turned to the musicians. "Take five."

Holding up a pitcher of ice water, he offered her some before pouring. At her refusal, he tipped up the glass and took a long pull, then hauled over a stool for her.

Most of the men Jordan knew fell into two categories. The ones who respected her position and dealt with her on a professional level, and the ones who flirted outrageously. Randy fit into the first category, although she also considered him to be in a class by himself. He was a friend.

When she was younger, she used to tag along after Clint and his friends like their shadow. Many summer afternoons were spent on the wide porch steps, sharing her cookies and milk with Randy and the others after the guys had played a vigorous game of touch football.

"I'm sorry I couldn't get over here sooner. I had a lot of cleaning up to do in the office."

"That's okay, J.D. I'm not going anyplace."

She smiled at his lazy drawl. "What did you want to see me about?"

"I thought you ought to look into getting an alternate date for our recording session."

She raised an eyebrow. "That's impossible. The studio is already leased. Why should we need a second date?"

He spoke softly, so the others wouldn't overhear. "I don't think Clint's going to be ready in time."

Surprise showed on her face. "Randy, he's only going to be gone for a few days. A week at the most." She studied him carefully. "Or do you know something I don't?"

Randy drummed his fingertips on the music stand, considering. Then his hands went still and he met her steady gaze.

"J.D. Personally, I don't think Clint will have the songs completed in time. He's going through some sort of personal crisis. He isn't able to concentrate on his music."

"But up at the farm..."

"The problems will still be with him. Don't you see? He's carrying them here." Randy touched a finger to his temple. "And here." He rested his hand near his heart.

She bit her lip. "Isn't there anything we can do?"

Randy shrugged. "All I can do is stand by and wait. This is one problem Clint has to solve without me." He paused. "But you, on the other hand..."

She clutched his sleeve. "What can I do, Randy?"

He stared deeply into her eyes, marveling at the innocence revealed in her gaze. There was no mistaking the sincerity of her question.

His voice softened. "Artists are often insecure in their...personal relationships."

He watched disbelief appear on her face. "Come on, Randy. I've watched the hordes of women fawning all over Clint after a performance."

"But fans are different. They're only infatuated with the idea of being near a celebrity. Clint knows that has nothing to do with him personally. In his private life, he never allows anyone to get close to him. Except for his brothers, and me...and you."

He noticed her hands clench together in her lap.

"I'd be a fool to think I could be important in Clint's life."

"Why?" He was watching her intently.

She shrugged. "I used to daydream..." She seemed to catch herself.

"Men daydream too, J.D."

She looked away. "Why are you saying this now, Randy?"

"Because I've seen the way you look at him. And I've seen the way he looks at you, when he thinks no one is noticing."

"The way he..."

"Clint can't take his eyes off you. There's a look, Jordy, when people are in love."

"Love." She made a bleak sound that she hoped would pass for a laugh. "Aren't you confusing love with lust?"

He heard the bitterness in her voice and reached out a hand to her shoulder. "Look at me, Jordy."

She met his steady gaze.

"I've heard some of the stories about Marty."

She flinched at the mention of her late husband.

"I guess I probably don't know half of what he did. But I can understand why you'd have a hard time trusting again."

As she opened her mouth, he interrupted. "I don't know what's been said between you, but I know Clint well enough to know when he's not faking it. The guy is heartsick, Jordy. And I'm honestly worried about him."

She couldn't speak. Her eyes rounded.

Randy watched the play of emotions on her expressive face.

Love. Could Clint love her? Was that why he had fled? She thought about the day before, in the school parking lot. He hadn't touched her. She had practically begged him with her eyes, and he had calmly held her car door.

Hadn't she told him she would love on her terms? She would decide whom to love, and when. And in return, he had given her a promise. She would never have to fight him again.

Clint was waiting for her to set the terms.

Leaping quickly from the stool, she turned with a nervous smile.

"Well, I'll look into a couple of alternate dates for the studio." She glanced up to find Randy still studying her.

What could she possibly say to this dear friend? She had no idea how everything would turn out. But he had opened a door.

She squeezed his hand. "Thanks, Randy."

He nodded.

With a quick wave to the musicians, she hurried from the rehearsal hall.

Back at the office, Jordan dialed the number of the farm. She told herself that she needed to hear Clint's voice, to reassure herself that he was all right.

While the phone rang, she drummed her fingertips on the desk. Randy was making too much of this. Everyone needed to get away once in a while. Single-handedly Clint bore all the pressures of the business. It was he who wrote the lyrics and the music, and arranged all the scores; it was Clint who hired and fired, who made all the final decisions on songs to be recorded on the album. He approved the technicians, photographers and even the cover art. The pressures of the business were getting to him. That was all.

Frustrated, she dropped the receiver. He was probably just out walking the dogs. She would try later. With a sigh of frustration, she turned to the pile of bills. Working with figures always took her mind off her problems.

By late afternoon, Jordan had dialed the farm's number at least a dozen times. By sheer determination, she managed to clean up all the work in the office. After one last attempt to reach Clint, she pulled the shades, locked the office door and headed for her apartment.

She spent the evening dialing the number of the farm. Where was Clint? Curiosity was giving way to concern. It was impossible to watch television. She picked up a book, discarded it. Prowling about the room, she began to imagine a hundred different things that could go wrong in the isolation of the country.

He'd taken a bad fall somewhere, out among the barren hills. There was no one to hear his calls. He'd cut himself on a tool and was bleeding to death on the floor of the barn. Her heart froze. A fire. No. Stop this. The phone was working. Her wild imagination continued to torment her.

She couldn't go to sleep until she knew Clint was all right. She just needed to hear his voice, she assured herself. Then, she could relax.

It was nearly midnight when she last dialed the number at the farm. The phone rang twice, three times. Her mind raced with all sorts of unimaginable terrors.

"Hello?"

At the sound of Clint's deep voice, her heart skipped several beats before returning to its natural rhythm.

"Oh, Clint. I've been so worried. Where have you been?"

"Jordy." She could hear the warmth in his tone. "Out walking most of the day. I needed to get out of the house. So I decided to walk over my property, get reacquainted with the land. It was wonderful.''

''How are the songs coming?''

His tone hardened. ''They're not.''

''What does that mean?''

''It means I seem to have gone dry. I haven't managed to write a thing since I got here.''

''Are you going to stay there?''

She listened to the long silence. ''I suppose so. I don't know where else to go. I don't think it matters where I am, I just haven't got it. The words are gone. The music has disappeared. I don't have a single inspiration left.''

Jordan smoothed the blanket of her bed and leaned back against the pillow. ''I wish there was something I could do, Clint.''

''There's nothing anyone can do. It's something I'll just have to work out by myself. But I'm glad you called, Jordy. It's good to hear your voice.''

''When you didn't answer the phone all day, I started to get a little crazy, I guess. I've been imagining all sorts of terrible things happening to you.''

She heard the sound of his muffled laughter. He stroked his beard. ''Well, even though I look pretty wild by now, life is far from primitive out here. I really do have all the conveniences of modern living. If anything happens to me, I can always phone for help. Besides, there are a few distant neighbours who look in on me from time to time.''

''I'm glad. I don't like to think about you all alone, driving yourself crazy over some song lyrics.''

A silence stretched between them. Neither of them wanted to end the conversation.

"What are you doing right now, Jordy?"

"Lying on the bed. Staring at the ceiling."

"So am I." His voice warmed. "Outside the window, there's a full moon. Little wispy clouds are blowing across the face of it right now. The night is so still. No traffic sounds. No sirens piercing the quiet."

She was silent.

"Do you remember, Jordy?"

Her voice was soft, hesitant. "I remember."

"It's so good up here. So peaceful."

"I'm glad you have the farm to go to, Clint. It must be wonderful to know it's there for you, whenever you need that solitude."

"Umm. It's my escape from life in the fast lane."

"Well." She sat up, wishing she could keep him on the phone all night. "I'd better let you sleep. If you've been walking your land all day, you must be half dead."

"No. I'm wide awake now." He paused. "Jordy, thanks for calling. I needed to hear your voice."

"Then maybe I'll call again. When I get to worrying about whether or not you're all right."

"Do that." He rubbed his beard. "Oh, Jordy. I wish you were here."

"You mean, you have to do your own dishes and laundry, and you wish you had someone to share the chores?"

He laughed. "That too." His voice grew serious. "No. I've never felt the loneliness like I do this time."

Her heart contracted. "I could tell you a lot about loneliness."

"Jordy..."

She waited, her eyes squeezed tight, hoping.

"Never mind. Sleep well."

She swallowed. "Good night, Clint."

She hung up the phone, and lay back against the pillow, with her hand flung over her face. She couldn't decide if the phone call had made it better or worse. Hearing his voice only made her more aware than ever of how much she missed him.

The next morning, as she woke to bright sunlight, she wondered if she'd only dreamed the conversation with Clint. She sat up. No. They had talked. But they had really said nothing. He was still at the farm, struggling with songs that refused to be born, and she was still here, trying desperately to ignore the feelings that stirred deep within her.

She dressed quickly, and hurried to the office. As she busied herself with the routine morning duties, she struggled with the images that kept drifting into her mind, distracting her.

Randy seemed to think that she could help Clint. Could she? Or would it only make everything worse if she went to him? He couldn't possibly understand what he was asking of her. What did he know of her dreams—her fears? How long had she been forced to ignore her dreams in order to take care of other people's needs? It seemed that all her life, someone had needed her. And she had always been there for them. Her parents, Clint's parents, Marty.

She frowned, and dropped the pile of mail to answer the phone. After jotting a note quickly, she picked up the mail and continued her work.

One selfish man, who cared only about his own needs, was enough for a lifetime. It was so much simpler this way. To live alone. To care for her own needs. She finally had a chance to think about herself. To love again, especially to love a dreamer who would always be chasing after rainbows, would invite disaster. Why should she set herself up for another heartbreak? No. She angrily tossed the mail down on the desk and poured herself a cup of coffee.

Randy should never have planted the seed of doubt in her mind. Now she was beginning to believe that she could make a difference in Clint's life. Only a fool would believe something like that. A man like Clint. He could have any woman he desired. And probably did.

If she went to him, and of course she wasn't planning such a foolhardy thing, she would have to do it with her eyes open. With the knowledge that he would probably accept her offering of love, but only because right now, he was feeling lonely and desperate. Once he got his life back in order, once the songs were completed, he would get back on track. And he would no longer need her.

Could she live life on such terms? Could she calmly walk into his life, offer him her love for as long as he wanted it, and then, just as calmly walk away?

She felt a tightness around her heart. No, she wouldn't do it calmly. But she could do it. She could do it for Clint's sake. Because, despite all her denials, she loved him. If her love could help him, even for a brief time, she had to offer it.

Jordan dumped the coffee down the sink and hurried to finish her work. She had to stop thinking. She needed to stay busy. Still, her mind refused to let go.

Since Marty's death, the one thing that had kept her going was the knowledge that she had no one but herself to depend on. At first, that thought had terrified her. But gradually, she had taken pride in her independence. Now, it was as important to her as life itself.

Jordan had developed a strong sense of who she was and where she was going. No one intimidated her. That was why she'd had the courage to approach Clint for the job as manager of his band. She knew she could do a better job than Marty had done. But along with her independence, there was an underlying fear of letting anyone get so close that he could impose his will on her. It had taken her a long time to feel whole again. No one, she vowed, would ever claim even a small part of her again.

Randy's words rang in her mind. "Clint is heartsick, Jordy. I'm honestly worried about him."

She pressed her palms to her feverish cheeks. What was happening to her? Only a fool would take another chance on love.

Chapter Seven

Before rush-hour traffic clogged the streets of Nashville, Jordan had tossed a few clothes into a suitcase and headed her battered car out of town.

Driving west on U.S. 40, she passed Belle Meade and the luxuriously beautiful homes of the affluent. Clint could have commissioned an architect to design a similar mansion, complete with pool, cars and all the trappings of success. Yet, for the most part, he shunned these displays, intent on his privacy, needing to return to his roots.

A lump formed in her throat at the road signs, as she drew nearer to her destination. Henderson County. It was the first reminder that she was actually heading home.

"I'm not afraid," she whispered, swallowing back the knot of fear. "I'll just make sure Clint is all right, and report the good news back to Randy."

The terrain, though still hilly, was less rocky here. The land was rich, full of promise. Jordan glanced at the dirt roads carved in the hillsides. The rusted hulk of an ancient truck, long forgotten by its owner, lay in a gully. Soon, the verdant summer vines would cover it completely. And always, standing guard along the highway, were those majestic columns of ledgerock, keeping their silent sentinel.

As the car sped along the highway, Jordan enjoyed the view. White fences undulated over gentle slopes of earth, defining prosperous farmland. Silver-capped silos stood watch over red barns and whitewashed outbuildings. Jordan looked beyond the buildings to the neatly harvested soil, lying dormant until the early spring plowing.

The air whistling past the car's windows held the bite of winter's moisture.

As she turned onto a dirt road, she paused, to allow a string of cows to pass. Their tails switched as they hurried toward the shelter of the barn on the other side of the road.

Chickens, finding a hole in the fence, scratched in the grass alongside the road.

The land here was tiered, the highest section set aside for the houses and outbuildings, the lower, bottom land, rich for farming, planted with crops. In winter the cattle grazed here, then, each evening, climbing the slopes, followed the road back to their familiar barn.

The lump in her throat was growing, threatening to choke her. This was the land of her childhood. How many years had she denied herself the pleasure of this trip? How many times had she thought of the farm, and the Donner family—and Clint?

She turned the car onto the single dirt lane that led to the farm and slowed, to savor all the wonderful sights and smells that were washing over her.

Here was the start of the fence that separated the Donner property from her family's land. Her father's dream had been to work this land. She felt a shaft of pain. But he had died without ever seeing the dream come true.

Jordan's hands gripped the wheel. She was more terrified now than she had been at thirteen, when she had first approached this house.

Ma Donner had promised her a cozy haven with her four boys. But to Jordan, boys were little creatures, like herself. And these giants who faced her across the room were men. They stared at her as if she had just arrived from another planet. And then wonder of wonders, one of them had winked at her, probably just to put her at ease. But at that lopsided grin, her heart had fluttered, then leaped to her throat. She bit her lip. That was where it seemed to be permanently lodged whenever she thought about Clint.

As she swung the car up the circular drive, she came to a halt near the freshly painted steps. Her gaze locked on the giant tulip poplar standing guard at the side of the porch.

Pa Donner had made her a swing out of a discarded tractor tire. One time Clint had pushed her so hard, she thought she'd fly over the top of the house. At her squeals of delight, he had pushed her harder and harder, until Pa had come out of the house, yelling at the top of his lungs for Clint to stop. On reflection, she realized that Clint had already been a man by then. He had consented to act like a silly schoolboy that day for her sake.

She passed a hand across her brow. How many times had he been forced to put aside his needs while he waited for her to grow up?

Jordan lifted her suitcase from the back seat and climbed the steps. Her knocks were met with a resounding silence.

She tried the front door. It opened. Inside, she stared around, feeling the years melt away.

The house was spacious, with oversize windows, sporting cushioned window seats. Bare hardwood floors were polished to a high sheen. Much of the furniture consisted of the original Donner antiques that she remembered. But many of the pieces were new, and obviously expensive.

Bookshelves had been built along one wall of the living room. She dropped her suitcase and crossed the room, running her hand along the leather bindings, skimming the titles. Shakespeare, Burns, the collected works of Frost. These must have been brought here to feed the hunger of the poet.

She studied the paintings and recognized among them a Remington, which had been in the family for years, and several new local artists she was familiar with. Clint would understand the need to encourage local talent.

A steady pounding from the backyard arrested her attention. She peered through the sheer gauze curtain and caught her breath at the sight of Clint, chopping wood.

His flannel shirt fluttered from the branch of a tree. Naked to the waist, he swung the ax with both hands in a neat arc above his head, and dropped the blade deep into the log. Sweat glinted between his shoulder blades. She studied the faded jeans that rode low on his hips. Her mouth went dry.

Late-afternoon sunlight slanted through the leaves of the tree, bathing him in its glow. His hair glistened darkly against his forehead and neck.

Jordan watched in fascination as he again lifted the ax above his head. The muscles of his arms and shoulders rippled with the motion, and she felt a contraction deep inside her. As the blade bit the wood, she clutched her arms about herself, then turned away.

She hadn't wanted to face it until now. She had pretended that she only wanted to assure herself that Clint was fine, that he was working on his music. It was time to end the lie. She did care about Clint. She did need to know that he was well. But the real reason she had come to the farm was to be with him. For as long as he needed her. She longed to feel those arms around her.

If Randy was right, if Clint loved her... Whether he did or not, she knew she loved him. She loved him as she had never loved anyone in her life.

She picked up the suitcase and climbed the stairs.

* * *

Clint dropped the ax. It had felt good to chop wood. It occurred to him that he liked to feel the calluses on his hands. He had grown up accustomed to doing hard farm chores. Even now, he didn't like it when his hands got too soft. He needed the physical release of hard work.

He carried the load of logs up the back steps, and shoved the door with his shoulder. Inside, he crossed to the huge living room, and dropped the wood alongside the fireplace. Wiping his hands on his jeans, he straightened.

Jordy. He could smell her perfume, here in the room. He must be going crazy. Pretty soon, he'd be talking to ghosts.

Kneeling, he tossed several logs on the grate, then added kindling. Tearing several sheets of newspaper, he lit them, waited until the kindling caught, then sat back on his heels, lighting a cigarette from the strip of paper, just seconds before it burned too close to his fingers. With a little oath, he dropped the torch into the fire and closed the screen.

He drew deeply on the cigarette, and watched the smoke curl upward. If only Jordy were here to share this fire. The house seemed emptier than he could ever recall.

He strode outside for another load of logs. Pulling on his shirt, he loaded up his arms, and with the cigarette dangling from his lips, climbed the steps and deposited the wood in a box beneath the window.

He turned, and for the first time caught sight of the sun glinting off Jordan's car in the driveway. He flipped the cigarette into the fire, then ran to the door and opened it wide. The car was empty. He closed the door and bounded to the stairs. As he reached the landing, he could hear the sound of water.

Clint followed the sound to Jordy's old bedroom. He stepped inside.

How many times had he walked into this empty bedroom and felt her presence here? It was the only room that he hadn't allowed himself to change. It was a little girl's room, with framed prints of ballerinas and kittens. A teenaged girl's room, with a red velvet, heart-shaped treasure box on a white dresser scarf. It was a woman's room, with the scent of her perfume lingering seductively in the air.

On the bed lay a drift of ivory silk that was probably meant to be a nightgown. Not wanting to soil it, he tentatively reached out the index finger of each hand and lifted it by the narrow straps. He felt his blood rush. It was only a few inches of lace and silk. It would cover nothing. He set it down, and allowed his gaze to trail to the black kimono beside it. He couldn't believe Jordy still had this. He had sent it to her years ago, when he was in the service.

He glanced at the suitcase, standing open on the floor. Had she come to stay?

For long moments, he stood by the bed, listening to the sound of the shower. His fists clenched and unclenched. He fought down the desire to rip open the bathroom door. Patience had never been one of his virtues. But this was Jordy's show, he reminded himself. He'd wait it out.

Clint walked to his room and stripped off his clothes. As he stepped beneath the shower, he reminded himself of his promise to her.

While he toweled himself dry, he thought about Jordy. It was impossible to think of anything else. He longed to run his fingers through that wild tangle of gypsy hair, to bury his face in it. It would be the sweetest torture of his life to see her in that little bit of ivory silk, covered by the kimono he had bought her so many years ago. Would he be able to keep from tearing them off her?

While he pulled on a clean pair of jeans, he stopped to peer at his reflection in the mirror. The shaggy growth of beard startled him. Why hadn't he bothered to shave? Now it was too late. He was thirty-three years old, and suddenly feeling like a sixteen-year-old on his first date. His blood was pounding. What had she done to him?

She was so strong, so determined. Yet he could sense her vulnerability. His jaw tightened. She deserved to be showered with love and tenderness. He wanted only the best for Jordy.

As he finished buttoning his shirt, he realized he was all thumbs. That little witch! She had him all tied up in knots. What was he going to say to her, when he saw her downstairs? How would she react? Cool and distant? Were they going to go on playing the part of employer and employee? Just good friends? Lovers? His heart beat double-time in his chest.

She was here with him. Here at the farm. For now, that was enough. He would try not to rush her. She could call all the shots.

He walked back downstairs, and added another log to the fire. As he straightened, he heard her footstep on the stairs. He turned his head, and caught his breath at the sight of her.

She had left her dark hair pinned up from the shower. Damp tendrils drifted about her face and neck. With her hair up, she looked cool and regal, as composed as any queen holding court. Clint's gaze trailed the pale column of her throat, exposed beneath the black kimono. He thought he detected a trace of ivory silk—or was it skin? His stomach muscles tightened.

"You were chopping wood when I got here. So I just decided to make myself at home." She took the last three steps with light little bounds and walked toward him.

"All the time I was working off my tensions out there, I was thinking how nice it would be to share this fire." He realized that she was barefoot.

"Then I'm glad to oblige." She stopped beside him, and gave him a radiant smile.

All the things she had planned to say and do were forgotten now that she was so close. She had waited so long. Dreamed and schemed, and thought her chance for love had passed her by. Was she trembling? She hoped it wouldn't show. Her throat went dry. Her heart was beating a wild tattoo in her chest.

"Will you stay for dinner?"

She stared up into his eyes, and wondered if that hunger had always been there. How could she have been so blind? "I don't think I'm interested in food right now."

"Good. Neither am I." He hooked his thumbs into his back pockets. "What made you decide to come out to the farm today, Jordy?"

"I thought you could use some company." She ran a fingertip along his arm and felt him tremble.

She felt a rush of courage. "I think I like your beard. It makes you look dangerous . . . primitive."

He was bewildered. This was a new part she was playing. He stared down at her. Her eyes glowed. Her lips parted in a smile. She was teasing, tempting.

He took a step back, uncertain how to deal with this new Jordy. "Would you like to hear some of the songs I've been trying to work on?"

"Maybe later." She stepped closer, and moved a hand up his chest.

He caught her hand. She slid the other along his arm. He pinned both of her hands between his, effectively stopping their movement. "Jordy, what the hell are you up to?"

"I'm turning the tables, Mr. Donner. What's the matter? Don't you like it?"

He stared down at her a moment, his eyes narrowed. "This isn't funny, Jordy. Do you know what you're doing to me?"

"Oh. Thank goodness! I was beginning to think I was doing this wrong." She laughed, and snuggled closer, lifting her mouth to his.

He stiffened. His breath seemed to have died in his chest. He couldn't breathe. Desire ripped through him, shattering his carefully planned control.

"Clint, I want you to kiss me." Her voice was low, seductive.

"Damn!" He let go of her hands, and dropped clenched fists to his sides.

"Does that mean no?" She chuckled.

He stepped back a pace. At his retreat, she grew bolder. Standing on tiptoe, she lifted her hands to his shoulders, and brought her lips to his throat.

She felt his quick intake of breath, felt the pounding of his pulsebeat. It quickened her own.

"I see that you're not going to make this easy for me. Ah, well, I've always wanted to undress the cool Clint Donner." Her fingers reached for the top button of his shirt.

Immediately, his hands closed around hers. His voice was thick with a passion that was about to explode. "Another game, Jordy? I can't play anymore. Don't push me any further."

Her voice coaxed. "Hold me, Clint."

She held her breath at the silence.

"If I hold you, Jordy, you can't tell me to stop. This time, there's no turning back."

"I knew that when I walked in the front door."

The silence between them was deafening.

He stared in amazement. For long moments, the only sound in the room was the hiss of flames in the fireplace.

Ever so slowly, his hands went to her hair, and with a twist of the clip, the silken strands drifted about her shoulders. He cupped her face in his hands, then allowed his fingers to play through the soft tangles.

"I don't want to hurt you, Jordy."

His arms were coming around her, drawing her inexorably to him.

"You can't, Clint."

But in a distant part of her mind came the realization that he was the only man who could hurt her. He was the only one with the ability to break her heart. She brushed it aside. Not now. She wouldn't think about that now.

"Oh, God, Jordy. How long. How long I've waited." His voice was muffled against her skin.

His mouth moved over hers, tasting deeply, taking her beyond thought.

His lips roamed her cheek, her eyelids, her temple, then came back to her mouth with new hunger. It wasn't enough. He couldn't get enough of her.

Her skin was hot where he touched her. She felt a raging need to touch him everywhere.

She didn't remember his hands sliding the kimono from her shoulders. She knew only his lips, following the ivory silk teddy, from shoulder to breast.

Her fingers fumbled with the buttons of his shirt. She gave a little moan of impatience. She wanted to tear it from him. Before, she had been so cool. Now she was caught up in a passion so intense, she could no longer think, only feel. She was grateful when she felt his fingers assist her with the buttons and snaps.

He had wanted to see how she would look in the ivory silk. But that was before this white-hot passion blinded him. Now his eyes saw only light. She was the light. And his rough fingers slipped the silk from her shoulders, sending her teddy to join the clothes on the floor.

He eased her gently to the floor. Then, with the last barriers gone, he lay beside her, cradling her in his arms. His lips moved over hers, drinking deeply, until her breathing was ragged. He brushed his lips over her throat, sending tiny shivers trembling through her body. His mouth moved over her breast, causing contractions to begin deep inside her. Her body had become a mass of nerve endings.

Searing, blinding heat was consuming them both. When his lips moved to her other breast, she arched her body to his, needing more, needing release.

Clint was beyond all thought. He was caught up in a need so intense he was on a razor's edge of sanity. Her moans, her hands moving on him, her lips fueled the fire. There was only Jordy. Her perfume enveloped him. Her scent was inside him.

He took her almost savagely. She clung to him, and moved with him, strong and sure, needing to match his rhythm, needing him as much as he needed her.

She was losing herself in him. Bits and pieces of herself seemed to drift and merge, until she was one with him. One, moving, lost in love, love so bright she felt they were floating toward a fire as intense as the sun. And then they were the fire. And it consumed them. She shuddered violently.

She felt his damp face pressed into a tangle of hair at her temple. His breathing was still hot and ragged. Her own was just as erratic.

His arms encircled her, holding her against him. She snuggled against his chest, and pressed her lips to the steady heartbeat.

When their pulse rates had returned to normal, he lifted himself on one elbow. Brushing away a strand of hair, he traced the outline of her face with a fingertip.

"Jordy. You're so special. I never wanted it to be like this."

When she looked at him, he saw a flicker of pain in her eyes. "You're . . . disappointed."

"In you?" He couldn't believe her question. "Jordy, you're more than any man could ever want."

Any man but Marty, she thought. She had never been enough for him. There had been so many women she had stopped counting.

Clint caught her chin, watching her struggle with the pain.

"I only meant I've wanted you for so long, that when I finally had the chance to love you, I lost control."

The look of pain disappeared. She brightened, then raised herself up to kiss his lips. "I've decided I definitely like you when you lose control, Mr. Donner." She smiled gently at his look of self-contempt. "You weren't the only one, in case you didn't notice. I wasn't exactly Miss Iceberg just now."

"I just mean that I wanted our first time to be slow and gentle, and instead, I took you right here on the floor like a madman."

"Then I see only one way for you to make it up to me."

He raised one eyebrow. "How?"

"You'll have to love me again. All night long in fact. And this time, in a proper bed."

He threw back his head in a roar of laughter. "I think my brothers were right about you all those years ago."

"What did they say about me?" She slid her hands down his chest, watching his eyes narrow at her touch.

"They worried that maybe the Gypsies dropped you on our doorstep. And that some day you'd cast a spell over us."

She moved her hands lower, and felt him catch his breath. "And what do you think?"

His eyes seemed to glaze at her touch. It was incredible that he could want her again, that he could need anyone this much. "Lady, I think I like falling under your spell."

He pulled her to her feet and lifted her in his arms. "Come on. There's a second fireplace in my bedroom. And a wonderful old four-poster bed."

Chapter Eight

It was the hushed, silken silence just before dawn. In the tulip poplar outside the window, no bird was yet chirping. In the rolling hills that ringed the farm, no cow was lowing.

Clint shifted slightly, to get a better view of the delicate creature who lay curled beside him. She was so beautiful, she took his breath away. A mass of tangled waves curved about one shoulder and drifted over her breast. A veil of dark hair fell over one eye seductively. He lifted the hair, and bent to touch his lips to her eyelid.

He watched her dark lashes flutter, then open. For one brief moment, he saw confusion in her eyes. Then she smiled, and he was being drawn again into that cool green light of her gaze.

"Good morning." He brushed his lips lightly over hers.

"Umm. Yes, it is." She ran a hand through her hair, and brushed the last strands from her neck, remembering their night of lovemaking. "Did I just dream last night, Clint?"

"If you did, I hope you never wake up." His fingertips began tracing the outline of her face, from her temple to her cheek to the curve of her jaw.

He had never known a night like this. They had loved with a frenzy that seemed to renew itself each time they came together, or even touched. They would doze, then reach out for each other, and the flame would burn anew.

She moved catlike against his hand, loving the feel of his work-roughened fingers against her skin.

"Has the fire burned down?"

He chuckled. "I'm afraid this is one fire that's never going to die, Jordy."

Laughter crinkled the corners of her eyes. "I meant the one in the fireplace."

"That one's still going strong, too."

She sat up in his arms. A log crackled invitingly on the grate.

"Umm. Can you think of anything more luxurious than a cozy fire and a big old soft bed?"

He pulled her gently down against the pillows. "That depends on who's sharing the bed." His hand slid across the flare of her hip, then moved to her slender waist, before gliding upward, toward the swell of her breast.

He saw her eyes soften and glaze slightly at his touch. Her lips parted for his kiss. He moaned softly against her mouth, while his fingertips gently explored the body he had begun to know as intimately as his own.

She pressed her lips to his hair-roughened chest, and felt his heartbeat leap at her touch. It excited her to know that she could have such power over him. Slowly, she brought her lips lower, and felt his stomach muscles contract violently. His reaction to her touch made her bolder, until her lips and hands moved lower still, working their magic, bringing him to a fever pitch.

He'd never known such desire. It was constant. It was insatiable. She was like a drug. The more he had of her, the more he wanted. While he had watched her sleep, he had promised himself that this time he would go slower, and savor each touch. But the moment he held her, the moment he felt her caresses on his body, his need became a primal scream, fighting for release.

He rolled over her, pinning her beneath his weight. Burying his face in the hollow of her neck, he murmured against her throat, "I can't believe what's happened to me. I have to have you, Jordy. Now."

Her voice was muffled and breathless against his ear. "I know, Clint. It's the same for me."

A fierce strength seemed to drive them, higher and higher, and then they were weightless, drifting, merging, then drifting again, until they lay, still locked as one, damp and breathless, clinging to each other's strength.

While the first pink flush of dawn lightened a sky shot with streaks of crimson, they slept.

When Jordan woke again, the sun was high in the sky. A fresh log had been added to the fire. It hissed as the flames split the bark, releasing the sap.

Clint lounged on the padded window seat, softly strumming his guitar. Barefoot, bare chested, he was wearing only a pair of jeans that rode low on his hips.

She lay very still for a moment, allowing herself to drink in the sight of him. Shaggy hair spilled across his forehead as he bent toward the strings, lost in thoughts of some unsung melody. He had shaved his beard. His features were smooth and even in the sunlight. She watched the muscles of his forearms flex and unflex as he strummed. Her hands clenched beneath the blanket. She loved the feel of those arms about her.

Did Clint realize what he had given her last night? In his arms, she had known the feeling of finally coming home. Home from a lifetime of wandering. Most of her life had been an incredibly exhausting journey. Home. It wasn't this farmhouse, or this old four-poster bed. It was this man. His embrace. His breath mingling with hers. His flesh heating hers. Clint Donner was the home her heart had been seeking all these long years.

Would he ever know what it had cost her to come to him? Or how many times she had thought about turning back? Yet, once she had walked through the front door, there was no retreating. If Randy was right, if Clint needed her as much as Randy had hinted, then it would have been worth any price. But the truth was, she had needed Clint's love even more.

How long was it since she had been held? How long, since she had felt the warmth of tenderness?

Still wrapped in a hazy glow, Jordan took the time to study her surroundings. Clint's bedroom had white stucco walls and a high, beamed ceiling. The sturdy oak beams gave the massive room a sense of strength and permanence. Yet because of the huge windows, framed with heavy oak molding and fitted with padded window seats, the room was also light and airy. Except for the touches of brown on the window seats and the comforter, everything in the room was white. The fireplace, which ran the length of one wall, was white granite, and sparkled in the sunlight. Two upholstered chairs, in brown-and-white plaid, flanked a round table of white marble. An antique desk in one corner spilled over with sheets of music. The bed was an antique four-poster, which had once been Clint's grandparents' bed. It was hand-carved from solid oak.

Spotting her movement, Clint set down his guitar and hurried across the thick white carpet to sit on the edge of the bed.

"Good morning, again." He brushed his lips over hers and felt the sudden sexual jolt.

"You shaved your beard." Jordan ran her fingers along his jaw, feeling the smooth texture of his skin.

"I thought I was enough of a barbarian last night to last a lifetime."

"I was beginning to like that shaggy, bearded face."

He caught her hand, and brought it to his lips. "Such long, slender fingers," he mused aloud. "Delicate. Jordy, you're so delicate."

She considered his words for a moment, then discarded them as a strange description. Chuckling, she said, "I've never thought of myself as delicate. Maybe I equate that with weak, and I've never thought of myself as weak."

"You're the strongest woman I've ever known." He planted a kiss in the palm of her hand, then curled her fingers over as if to hold his kiss. "Any man would love your strength." He regretted the remark the moment the words were out.

Instantly she stiffened, snatching her hand from his. She turned her face into the pillow, but not before he saw the pain. "Maybe some men. But some men resent it. Some men prefer weak women, who can be easily controlled. They'd probably rather have a trained pet who waits at the door with a pair of slippers in one hand and a drink in the other."

Agitated, she stood, completely unaware of her nakedness. Turning her face away, she nearly whispered, "I'm sorry, Clint. I've never said that aloud before."

He wanted to hold her, but he knew she needed to stand alone. He touched her shoulder. "Hungry?"

She nodded. The warmth of laughter came back to her eyes. "Do you realize that we skipped dinner last night? I'm starving."

"So am I." His gaze skimmed her. "Your robe is still downstairs on the floor, where I ravished you."

They both laughed.

"Here." He removed a velour robe from his closet. "You'll look lost in this, but it's warm."

She slipped into the rich burgundy-colored robe, and tied the sash, while Clint rolled the sleeves above her elbows.

He took her hand. "Come on. Let's see what we can throw together."

Downstairs, he drew open the vertical blinds, letting the morning light reveal a sparkling country kitchen.

"Clint. You've completely remodeled this room."

He nodded. "I left the brick fireplace, and the hardwood floor. But all the appliances are new. And I had one wall removed and replaced with a wall of glass doors, for easy access to the patio."

She stared around her, loving the clean, airy feeling of the old house. "It's lovely," she breathed. "But my stomach won't let me admire it until after I've eaten. How about an omelette?" she asked.

"Great. I'll make the toast."

Together, they worked about the kitchen in companionable comfort, until, within a short time, the table was set with a tempting breakfast.

"How are you coming on your songs?" Jordan asked, stirring cream into her coffee.

Clint shook his head. "I haven't been able to get a thing done. Too many distractions."

"And now I'm here, taking up more of your time."

"That's right." He bent and kissed her lips, then poured more coffee. "And you're definitely a distraction."

She made a face at him.

"Would you like me to arrange for a later recording date?"

He considered. "No, I think we're cutting it too close, Jordy. There are too many people involved. And some of them have other dates scheduled. I might end up having to hire new technicians, people I haven't worked with before. Let's just stick to the original date." He grinned at her over the rim of his cup. "Ill just have to force myself to concentrate on my work instead of play."

While they were loading the dishwasher, Jordan touched his arm. "Clint, look."

A squirrel did a high-wire act across the telephone line that ran from a pole to the house. There he climbed down and skittered among the leaves on the patio until he found a crust of bread. Leaping onto a wrought-iron patio chair, he curled his tail over his back and ate his breakfast in the morning sun. When he had finished, he climbed the side of the house, danced once more across the telephone line and headed for his home.

"Friend of yours?" she asked.

"Yes. It shows you how lonely I've been feeling lately. I've been tossing out scraps every day, hoping to entice him to do his number for my entertainment."

"Here." Jordan handed him a plate with some left over toast. "See that your friend isn't disappointed tomorrow."

The phone rang. Clint set down the plate and answered it while Jordan wiped the table. She looked up at his sharp tone. He was frowning.

"No. I haven't finished them yet. I've...been busy." His tone became sterner. "You can't come out here."

He listened. "I don't care. I'll take care of it when I get back. I've told you before, this place is off-limits. I conduct my business in Nashville."

While he continued speaking, Jordan dried her hands and walked out of the room. In the living room, she bent and picked up her kimono and teddy, and carefully folded Clint's clothes.

As she climbed the stairs, she was deep in thought. There was a time for work and a time for play. She was being selfish. There were too many people counting on Clint. He needed to devote all his time to his songwriting now if he was going to be ready for the recording session. She was a distraction. Her presence here would only hold him back. How could she have convinced herself that she was needed? She would only be in the way.

She stepped under the shower, and forced herself not to think of her empty apartment in Nashville.

She slipped on the ivory teddy, then stepped into jeans and buttoned up a cotton shirt. After closing her suitcase, she stood and flipped her hair back from her shoulders.

She took a last lingering look around Clint's room, before descending the stairs.

Clint tossed another log in the fireplace, then stood at the sound of her footsteps.

"What . . . ?" he stared at the suitcase. "Where do you think you're going?"

She forced her tone to remain light. "Time to get back to work."

"Jordy." He caught her by the shoulders, and felt her stiffen at his touch.

"You didn't say a thing about this at breakfast." He stared down at her.

She avoided his eyes. "I just assumed you knew. It's time for me to get back."

He was confused. He couldn't think. He didn't want her to leave. "Of course I didn't know. I thought you intended to stay with me."

"Be realistic, Clint. We both have work to do. I have an office to run. And you have some songs to write, if you intend to keep that recording date."

He studied her. She was avoiding his eyes. Something was wrong.

"Is it something I said? Something I did?"

She turned away, shaking her head. "Of course not, Clint. Really. I have to go now."

He caught her arm, but still she avoided his eyes. His voice lowered dangerously. "Damn it, Jordy, talk to me. Tell me what's going on."

She forced herself to face him. The pain in his eyes startled her. She wondered what he could read in hers. "That phone call reminded me just how selfish I've been, Clint. You have priorities. I'm not one of them. Right now, you have some songs to write. You're in a kind of limbo here, needing to finish the songs so you can record, and needing to hold everyone in Nashville back, so you can be alone to do that. I'm interfering."

"No!" He gripped her arms painfully. A smoldering fire flared in his eyes. "You've gone far enough."

"What?" She backed away, startled by his blazing anger.

He caught her by the shoulders. His strong hands began a rhythmic massage. "Jordy, you've insisted on having your own way. You said you would decide when to love, and whom. All right. Fair enough. I've given you your head. But no more. I don't know where you got the idea that you were in the way, but I need you here with me. I want you to go upstairs and unpack right now."

"But I..."

Desperation drove him. He would keep her here at any cost. "I couldn't think of anything but you while I was alone. You clouded my thoughts, kept me from my work. And now that you've come to me, you're staying. I need you here, do you understand? I need you, Jordy."

"I..." She licked her lips.

"And furthermore, forget that stupid promise I made. You'll have to fight me, Jordy, if you try to leave me."

She hesitated. "How will you write?"

He noted her hesitation and smiled. "I'll squeeze some writing time in between our loving."

"Oh, Clint." She sighed, and he drew her close.

"Don't ever think about leaving me, Jordy. I'm no good without you." His lips grazed her cheek, then pressed to her ear. His teeth lightly nipped her lobe, before his tongue flicked softly in her ear.

A heaviness seemed to pervade her limbs. As his lips moved to her throat, she arched her neck, knowing she should stop him now, but unwilling to end the pleasure his lips brought.

"I think I'm going to have to show you how very much I need you." He chuckled against her throat, sending ripples of pleasure along her spine. His voice became a low, throaty growl. "Now it's my turn to undress the very cool Jordan Hunter."

"Clint!"

His fingers found the buttons of her blouse, and he slowly unbuttoned it, then slipped it from her shoulders.

She seemed mesmerized by the fire in his dark eyes. She could only stare, her hands held limply at her sides, as he continued the seduction.

He unsnapped her jeans, and slid them over her hips. He was surprised to feel silk beneath the rough denim fabric. But then, that was typical of Jordy. The small, fragile-looking woman, who was as tough as nails. The street-smart little cookie, who cried at tender ballads. Silk and denim.

He held her a little away from him, and allowed his gaze to slowly skim her figure, clad in the ivory teddy.

"Yesterday, while you showered, I ached to see you in this. But last night I was too overcome to take the time to enjoy the sight. Now, Jordy, I intend to savor." His voice was liquid honey, pouring over her senses.

He bent his lips to her shoulder, and ran featherlight kisses across her tender skin. It excited him further, to feel the tremors his touch caused in her. He forced himself to go slowly.

His fingers caressed her thighs, then rose to her hips, where the teasing bit of lace rested. He felt her tremble at his touch.

His mouth covered hers, tasting, drawing deeply on her sweetness.

With his thumbs, he moved the straps over her shoulders and watched the silk slip across her breasts and down to her hips. His breath caught in his throat, and he fought down his need. He lowered his lips to a breast, and felt the convulsive shudder that passed through her.

"Oh, Clint. Hold me," she pleaded.

One arm encircled her, while his other hand continued to tease her taut breast. His mouth moved over hers, all the while nibbling, tasting. Her breath was coming faster now, as her heartbeat accelerated.

His hands moved down her body, until they found the ivory silk clinging to her hips. With a quick movement, he slipped the fabric over her hips and felt it drift to the floor.

In one fluid motion, he lifted her in his arms and carried her up the stairs. As he pressed her onto the pillows, she sighed. Clint had said she was strong. But now there was no strength left in her. He could do anything with her he wished. She had never known such a sweet weakness.

"Please, Clint. I want you now." Was that her voice begging? She had never begged before. But then, she had never wanted anything as much as she wanted him.

He removed his clothes. Lying beside her, he smiled. "I told you, Jordy. This time, I intend to savor."

His lips began burning a trail of kisses over her body. "You've been a fever in me for as long as I can remember."

She moaned, and felt the fire shooting through her veins.

"A fever that's been raging through me, Jordy. Draining me." His lips, his fingertips, were taking her beyond reason.

"Please, Clint. Now." She didn't recognize her own voice. It was a strangled whisper.

He lifted his head to study her eyes, which were glazed with passion. "Not yet, Jordy. Not until we can't wait another moment."

His lips found hers, moist and swollen from his kisses, trembling with the need for more.

And then his hands and lips began again their gentle exploration of her body.

"Umm. A strange place to dab your perfume, Jordy."

His voice was husky, as his lips trailed the cleft between her breasts.

His lips moved lower, circling her stomach, before dipping lower still.

She arched and moaned and whispered his name. Or did she only dream it? Her fingers twined in his hair, and she experienced a weakness she had never known before.

"Oh, Jordy," he murmured against her mouth. "Promise me you'll never leave me."

"I promise. For as long as you want me."

"You're all I've ever wanted."

He took her then, slowly, slowly, until she thought she would explode from wanting him.

And then the tenderness dissolved, and he crushed her to him, his mouth devouring hers, his body plundering hers, taking her higher, higher, until he felt her shuddering release.

So this was madness. This was the passion that had driven him beyond all reason. And now she was sharing his insanity. There was no cure for it. Only a brief respite, until the next time it rose to take over her careful control.

She cradled his damp face against her throat, feeling the draining weakness that seemed to have spread from her limbs to her entire body. Tiny tremors still rocked her.

He didn't move. His words were spoken against her skin. "There isn't any music without you, Jordy."

For long moments she didn't speak. He listened to her unsteady breathing, wondering if his body was pinning her too tightly to the mattress. He didn't want to move. It was heaven in her arms. But he knew he must be heavy on her.

He lifted himself slowly from her arms and glanced at her face. She was weeping.

"Jordy. I hurt you."

She shook her head, ashamed that he had caught her crying. "No. No, Clint. You didn't hurt me."

He touched her face, gently wiping the tears with his thumbs. "Don't cry, Jordy. What did I say? What did I do?"

She wiped a hand across her tears. "You said there was no music without me."

He was incredulous. "You mean you're crying because you're happy?"

She nodded, too overcome to speak.

He smiled gently, then brushed her lips softly with his. "It's true. This morning, when I woke, I could hear the song I've been trying for months to write. It was all there. Complete. Because of you." He drew her into his arms, and felt the warmth of her slowly seep into him. "That's why you have to stay with me, love. Stay with me and love me, be my music."

She buried her face in his neck. He could feel the dampness of her tears. She struggled to calm her ragged breathing. "I will, Clint. For as long as you want."

Chapter Nine

"I'm going for a walk. Want to come along?"

Clint had seemed restless all morning, as if he wanted to share something with her. But true to his word, he had worked on his music, while she busied herself elsewhere. Every hour he had come out of the huge den, where he labored at a grand piano. He would find her, stare at her while he pretended not to, prowl about the room, then return to the den for another hour of work.

Jordan looked up from her book. "Sure." She grabbed up a jacket and followed Clint from the house.

The barn was over a mile from the house. Ignoring the road, they climbed fences like carefree children and followed their own path over the rambling hills.

"The land looks like it was harvested," Jordan said, examining the neat furrows in the soil.

"It was."

"Who does the farming, Clint?"

He caught her hand, swinging it as they walked. "I hired a nice young couple who live on the adjoining farm to manage mine as well. They're doing a fine job. In exchange for managing my place, he gets the use of some of my property to grow his crops, and a share of the profits."

When they reached the barn, he gave her a mysterious smile. "Got a little surprise for you."

He threw open the door, and led her inside. As her eyes grew accustomed to the dimness, she spotted Clint's favorite hunting dog lying in the hay. And then, with a look of wonder, she realized the surprise.

"Oh, Clint. Mollie had puppies."

She bent to pet the dog, then knelt to stare at the squeaking little bundles of black and brown that poked out from beneath their mother.

For over an hour, they sat in the hay, examining each puppy, exclaiming over their big feet and floppy ears, cuddling, laughing over their antics as they tugged at their mother's ears, or tripped over each other, while the big black hunter looked on proudly.

"When they're old enough to be weaned, would you like one, Jordy?"

She was holding a tiny bundle to her heart, murmuring to it, as it licked her face. It was a tempting offer. Sadly she shook her head.

"I have no place for a dog in my crowded apartment, Clint. Besides, these are hunting dogs. They deserve lots of land to roam. It wouldn't be fair to give them to city people. You should keep them here in the country."

He nodded. "How come you're always so sensible, Jordy? You're right, you know. They belong here on the farm." His voice thickened with emotion. "So do you."

Deep in sleep, Jordan turned toward Clint, anticipating the warmth of his touch. Instead, the bed was cold. For a moment, her fingers brushed his pillow. Then she was instantly awake.

She lay for long moments, listening to the sound of music from the room below. Pulling on a robe, she padded downstairs. For a moment, she stood outside the door of the den, watching as Clint made notes on the paper lying on the piano. Then she stepped inside, as he sat down and began to play once more.

It was a haunting melody. Snuggling into the chair, Jordan tucked her feet underneath her and leaned her head back, letting the music wash over her.

Clint was a gifted songwriter. She had no doubts about his talents. And in the last few days, the music had begun to flow from him once again.

She never asked him to play for her, or to sing the words. She felt it would be an invasion of his privacy. If he volunteered to play for her, she was an enthusiastic audience. But when he went off to work, she found dozens of ways to stay busy, and out of his way.

He turned and for the first time became aware of her presence in the room.

"Jordy. I woke you."

"No. I woke myself." She smiled. "That song is beautiful, Clint."

He nodded. "I think it's becoming my favorite. I can't get it out of my mind."

"What's the title?"

"Wildflowers." He walked up and held out his hand. "Come on. It's cold down here."

"I don't feel cold." She accepted his hand and stood. "Aren't you going to stay here and work?"

The look he gave her sent her pulse racing. "No. I've just decided there's something else I'd rather be doing."

Together, they climbed the stairs to bed.

"Would you like to go out to dinner tonight, Jordy?"

She looked up. "Are you trying to tell me you're tired of my cooking?"

He laughed. "I love your cooking. It's almost as good as mine."

He had surprised her by being an excellent cook. The years on the road when he had been forced to eat in restaurants had taught him the value of learning how to cook for himself.

Jordan thought about the sameness of the menu at Will's diner, and the many times she wished she had more room in her cramped apartment kitchen to try some special meals.

"I'd really rather eat here, Clint. I thought I'd make you my famous spaghetti sauce tonight."

He gave her the lazy smile that never failed to excite her. "I was hoping you'd say that. I'd much rather share a simple meal with you here than drive into town to a restaurant.''

"I'd better check the supplies. I may need a few things from town.''

"I have to drive in for some things anyway. Give me a list.''

Jordan checked the kitchen cupboards, then jotted down the items she needed from the store.

Clint pulled on his jacket. "Sure you don't want to come with me?'' A mysterious smile played about his lips. He was planning a secret.

She decided to indulge him. "No. I'll start the sauce while you're gone.''

He kissed her firmly on the lips. "Do you realize this is the first time I've left you since you came here?''

"See that you don't leave me alone too long.'' She returned the kiss.

Standing in the doorway, she waved until he was out of sight.

Jordan got busy in the kitchen, adding all her secret ingredients to the iron skillet, seasoning, tasting, until the wonderful spicy aroma of spaghetti sauce filled the house.

She heard the slam of a car door, and hurried to open the front door for Clint. She stopped. She didn't recognize the car. And then a familiar figure strode briskly up the steps, and hesitated, staring at her as if seeing a ghost.

"Danny!''

His face lit with a smile.

"Jordy! Is it really you?''

They rushed together in a warm hug.

He held her a little away from him.

"My Lord. It isn't possible. You haven't changed at all."

She studied the friendly open face, so like Clint's. The same dark hair spilled in disarray about his forehead. His dark eyes were warm and friendly, his shoulders broad, and there was a slight thickening about his middle.

Danny was the oldest of the four brothers. And next to Clint, her favorite. He had always seemed like the father she had lost. He was gentle, simple and direct.

During his vacations from college, when he was at the farm, Jordan used to tag along after him, badgering him with a million questions. He never showed any impatience with her. And sometimes, as a special treat, he would allow her to hold a bird or animal while he tended its wounds. It was to this gentle man she had confided her fears, and on a rare occasion, her dreams.

He glanced around. "Isn't Clint home?"

"No. He's gone to town for some things. Come in, Danny." She beamed. "It's so good to see you again."

He followed her through the house to the kitchen. "Something smells wonderful."

"I'm making spaghetti sauce. You'll have to stay for dinner."

He shrugged. "Wish I could, Jordy. I have to be in Nashville for a medical society dinner tonight. I thought it was the perfect time to grab a visit with Clint."

"Clint tells me you're a country doctor now, Danny. He's so proud of you."

He grinned, the artless grin of the big, strapping youth she remembered. "Country doctoring suits me, don't you think?"

"Perfectly."

"It's all I ever wanted," he said simply.

She reached up to wrap her arms around his shoulders. For long, silent moments she pressed her cheek against his chest. Then she stepped back.

"Do you have time for a cup of coffee?"

"Sure. Sounds fine."

As she busied herself at the stove, she said, "I hear you almost had to quit medical school, Danny. Clint said you came into some money in time to finish."

Danny chuckled. "That sounds like Clint. I'll bet he didn't bother to tell you where the money came from."

She turned. "Why, no. I guess I didn't ask."

"The money was his. All he had saved from a year on the road." Danny shook his head, remembering. "At first, I thought it would be the lowest thing in the world to take his hard-earned savings. But I was desperate. And then, Clint told me that I was the reason he'd worked so hard. Because I'd always believed in him." He glanced up at Jordan. "Can you imagine?"

She assembled the coffeepot, then came to Danny, smiling. "Yes. I can imagine. The four of you have something special, Danny. You would have done the same for any one of your brothers. And you know it."

He nodded, studying her. "I guess you're right." He shifted. "Are you just here for the day, Jordy?"

She flushed. He had to be aware of her discomfort. "I'm ... staying here with Clint while he finishes the songs he's writing for his album."

His disapproval would cut deeply. She braced herself for the expected censure.

Instead, he smiled gently. "I'm glad."

Her lashes fluttered. She looked up to find him staring thoughtfully at her. "You are?"

She had the most open, honest face he had ever seen. In an instant, he detected her insecurity. He touched her arm. "Jordy, honey, Clint has needed you in his life for a long time."

She shook her head softly. "It seems that I'm the only one who wasn't aware of that fact."

They sat in silence until the kettle whistled, breaking the spell. Jordan rose and poured the boiling water in the pot. Within a few minutes she poured two cups of coffee and placed one in front of Danny. She sat across from him, thoughtfully stirring in cream.

He caught her hand and squeezed it. "I think being back at the farm agrees with you, Jordy. You look wonderful."

She smiled shyly, pleased by Danny's gentle acceptance of her. "I feel wonderful. Like I've been reborn."

His voice lowered. "I...know about Marty. At least I've heard a few things. You deserved better."

He saw her lips suddenly press together. He touched her hand. "You know, Jordy, when I was a kid tramping over the hills of our farm, I learned to spot an injured bird or animal by the way they held themselves."

As her eyes widened, he said gently, "When a bird has a broken wing, he tucks it close to his body, holding it so tightly, he thinks it doesn't show." Danny ran a hand through his hair in a familiar gesture. "I don't know. Maybe it hurts less that way. For whatever reason, he thinks it makes him look less vulnerable to predators." His eyes met hers. "But the poor little thing still can't fly."

She stared at the tabletop, avoiding his eyes.

He cleared his throat. "I don't think I can mend broken wings, or broken hearts. But maybe if you talk about it, I can try." His voice grew soft. "Why did you rush off and marry Marty?"

She pressed her hands to her cheeks, feeling a rush of heat at the question. She studied the man who had always been so kind to her. Did he realize how painful this was? She bit her lip. Maybe it was time to talk to someone. Despite the ghosts it would resurrect, she decided she needed to confide in a friend. And Danny had always been her friend.

"Why did I rush off and marry?" She sighed. "How many times have I asked myself that. After your dad died, I figured I'd better look for a job. Even though I was only seventeen, I'd graduated from high school and didn't know anything except being busy. Besides, a neighbor told me that the farm would probably be sold to a stranger, and the property divided among the four of you, unless one of you wanted to buy out the other three. That meant I'd need a place to live."

Danny nodded. "Glen drew up the papers at Pa's request. I think Pa always secretly hoped one of us would want to stay on at the farm. But we had all chosen our own paths by then." His voice warmed. "Of all his sons, I'll bet Pa never thought it would be Clint who would eventually decide to settle here."

Jordan agreed with a wry smile. "The Prodigal Son. Your Pa used to say Clint had gone off to the bright lights of the city for good."

Again, Danny noted the shadow of pain in her eyes.

She blinked, bringing her attention back to him. "Anyway, Danny, I knew it was time to make my own way. It was kind of your parents to take me in, but I didn't want to be a burden on the rest of you. I found a job at the record company. Marty worked there. He started asking all my friends about me, finding out all he could about my background. I was flattered. I thought here was a man who was just interested in me." Her voice deepened, and Danny realized how difficult this was for her.

"I'd never even dated a boy." She glanced at Danny. "After school, I always had to get home and take care of your dad. There wasn't time for dates. Besides..." Her voice trailed off, leaving him wondering what she might have said. Was it Clint, even then, who held her heart?

He waited patiently for Jordan to tell the story in her own way.

She sipped her coffee, avoiding Danny's eyes. "A week after I met him, I was married to Marty Hunter. He bought a big apartment, a flashy car and lots of new clothes."

She stood in agitation. "He told me I was the queen of his heart. And for the next four years, I let him control my life. He said what we would buy and when. He decided whether to go out or stay home." She shook her head, sending the dark hair dancing about her shoulders. "What a little fool I was. I very quickly learned I had lost my royal status."

"But why, Jordy?" Danny stood and touched a hand to her trembling shoulder. "A man like that."

She heard the disgust in his voice.

"Because I didn't know any better. At least in the beginning." She turned to face him. "I was so foolish. Did you know that when I turned twenty-one, Marty announced that I had come into an inheritance?"

Danny's eyes narrowed. "An inheritance, Jordy?"

"My parents' land. I don't know how Marty knew. I hadn't heard a word about it. Maybe he opened my mail." Her voice trembled. "Maybe he even checked it out at the county offices before he bothered to marry me." She shrugged. "I thought the land had been sold years earlier. I guess I'd been too young to wonder about it at the time of their deaths. And afterward, it just never occurred to me."

"What did you do with the land?" Danny almost hated to ask.

Her voice dropped. "Marty needed money. He owed a few people who weren't being very nice about waiting for their payments. So I signed some papers. Marty said he made a quick sale. Afterward, we moved to a bigger apartment. He bought a bigger car. And better clothes." She laughed bitterly. "So much for Marty's needs."

Danny's hand clenched at his side.

Her words told him little of the facts of her life with her husband. But the depth of the pain of that life was evident on her face.

She turned bleak eyes to Danny. "I used to wonder why Marty married me. Was it just because I was so easy to con? Or was there more? Did he know from the beginning about the land? Or did he want to use my connection with Clint to get a job as his manager? Every time I began to question his motives, he'd sweet talk me into believing him." Tears swam in her eyes. "Oh, Danny. I was so naive. I was in love with the idea of love. All I ever really wanted was..." She swallowed the words, hoping she hadn't said Clint's name aloud. "I threw it all away. And in the end, I found myself alone. Always alone."

"No children, Jordy?"

Again the pain, sharp, fleeting.

"I married a selfish child. He couldn't tolerate the competition."

His arms reached out for her, and she nearly went to him. Dear Danny. But she caught herself in time. She needed to be strong, not weak and whimpering.

"Don't get me wrong, Danny. I didn't wish Marty dead. But I had finally found the strength to make my own way. I would have left him. Our marriage was a farce. But he... died first."

Danny paused for a moment, wondering how much he should reveal. Then, taking a deep breath, he plunged in.

"Did you ever ask Marty how he got the job as Clint's manager?"

She shook her head. "I tried. He always put me off. But I heard him bragging to friends that he was just too good not to get noticed sooner or later by the top singers."

Danny raised an eyebrow. "That's slightly different from the version I got from Clint."

She stiffened.

"Clint told me that Marty came to him insisting that you needed money. He said, since you were practically family, that Clint should take care of his 'little sister.' Then Marty offered to be Clint's manager, in exchange for enough to keep you 'in comfort.'"

"Oh, I should have known." Her voice broke. "How could Clint believe such lies?"

"Maybe the same way you did, Jordy." Danny's voice was patient. "It didn't matter whether he believed Marty or not. If there was even a shred of truth in what Marty said, Clint had to do right by you."

"Me!" A simmering anger roughened her voice. "If Clint had cared about me all those years ago, he never would have left."

She fought back the tears that burned her throat.

Danny's voice was calm, even. "Clint never really left the farm, Jordy. His heart was always there—with you."

Her voice was a cry of pain. "I don't believe that." She struggled for calm. "Your pa said Clint had left for good. He told me that Clint had a right to chase his dreams, and that if we really loved him, we had to let him go completely."

Tears shimmered for a moment, then spilled down her cheeks. "And I knew the only way I could ever get

Clint out of my thoughts was to hurry up and make a life for myself apart from him."

She turned, and saw Clint standing in the doorway. How long had he been there? How much had he heard?

She brushed past him and ran from the house.

As Danny reached out a hand, Clint stopped him.

"Let her go, Danny. I know Jordy well enough to know she needs to cry alone."

"I shouldn't have asked her any questions." Danny shook his head in agitation. "I'm afraid I pushed her too far, Clint."

His brother's voice was soft. "Danny, you did something I never could have done. You got her to talk about something so painful, she couldn't even allow herself to think about it. Now, finally, maybe she can heal."

Danny stared anxiously out the window. "Where will she go?"

Clint's voice lowered. "If I know Jordy, she'll run and then walk, just keep moving until she's ready to drop. By the time she gets back here, she'll have worked out a lot of the pain and grief that's been burdening her for so long."

The two brothers watched in silence as the tiny figure disappeared over the hill.

Chapter Ten

The setting sun bled into the surrounding hills. Long ridges of mauve and crimson added fiery color to the drab winter landscape as she walked back toward the farmhouse.

What could she possibly say to Clint? She had been stunned to see him standing there in the doorway. How long had he been there? How much had he heard?

Her thoughts shifted to his brother. Dear, dear Danny. He had been more honest with her in that brief visit, than any of Marty's friends had been in all the years she had known them. Had everyone always been aware that he was a con artist? She dug her hands deeper into her pockets, hanging her head.

What a foolish child she had been. She had hung onto fairy tales for so long. She lifted her chin defiantly. She hadn't been the only one. Marty had managed to ply his trade on others. Her teeth clenched. She just stuck around to take it longer than most.

She drew her collar up around her neck, to ward off the chill. A new thought struck. Was she going to allow this latest knowledge of Marty to destroy all she had begun to build? After all, Clint didn't hold her responsible for Marty's actions. Clint had already known a good deal about her late husband. And still, he had taken her on as manager of his band. In the final analysis, it would be her work that mattered. This was her life now. She was in control of her own destiny. Her head lifted higher. She had set out to rebuild her world. She wouldn't look back again. Only forward.

At the door, she paused, took a deep breath, then stepped inside. Warmth enveloped her. Not just the warmth of the indoors, but the warmth of love that was evident all around her.

A fire crackled in the fireplace. In front of it, a round table had been set for two. On an antique lace tablecloth gleamed fine china and ornate silver. A low crystal bowl caught and reflected the light of the fire. In it were massed dozens of flowers. She gave a little exclamation of delight. Daisies, lilies and snapdragons gave off their delicate fragrance. There were purple irises and brilliant red poppies, soft blue cornflowers and palest pink carnations, delicate lacy ferns and baby's breath.

The only light in the room came from the fire, which cast flickering shadows about the corners of the room, and from several candles in antique silver candlesticks, which cast their soft glow on the table setting.

The wonderful spicy scent of her spaghetti sauce drifted from the kitchen, mingled with the scent of bread heating in the oven.

Clint came through the doorway, carrying a bottle of red wine. He had changed to dark slacks and a pale silk shirt that contrasted with his dark hair and eyes.

Seeing her, he set the wine bottle in an ice bucket, and hurried to take her cold hands in his.

"I hope you're hungry." His gaze roamed the wild mane of hair, the upturned collar. "I thought you might be glad of a fire."

Her eyes lowered for a moment, but not before he glimpsed her uncertainty. He fought down the need to draw her into his arms. He could sense her conflicting emotions. He would go slowly. She needed time.

"Yes, to both." Her voice sounded breathless. Was it from the long walk, or because of his nearness? "I'm starving, and I didn't realize how cold I was. I'm grateful for the fire."

She looked up to find him studying her closely. Avoiding his gaze, she walked to the table. "Where in the world did you find these flowers this time of year, Clint?" She bent her face to the intoxicating fragrance. "Umm. They're wonderful."

"That's what I went into town for. I ordered them as a surprise for you." He was watching her. "Don't you know what today is?"

She looked up from the bouquet, her eyes growing round. "No. What?"

"It's our anniversary."

"Our..."

"One week. For seven whole days now, I've been the happiest man in the world. I thought that was worth celebrating."

She started to laugh. "Now I know I'm in the presence of a madman."

"Well, thank you very much. But I'll accept that as a compliment, since I've decided that you're not completely sane yourself."

He bowed grandly before her, and saw the glint of laughter in her eyes. He relaxed. He could hold her now that he sensed her tension had dissolved. He smoothed a wayward strand of hair, then lifted her chin gently.

"Jordy, I'm glad you're back." His lips brushed hers lightly, and the familiar flame began flickering deep inside him. "This house is a tomb without you." His arms came around her, drawing her tightly to him. "Run as far as you like, Jordy. To the ends of the earth, if you need to. But always come back to me. I'll always be here." He drank more deeply from her lips.

She caught her breath. Would he? Hadn't he left all this far behind for a chance at the bright lights? For one brief moment she tensed, then she relaxed against him, pushing aside the doubts that plagued her, feeling the warmth of him spreading through her.

His lips moved over hers, and his arms tightened their hold on her, drawing her so close, she could feel his heartbeat matching her own.

He moved his lips along her cheek, then dipped his mouth to her throat. "While I toss the salad, why don't you go upstairs and change." His teeth nipped her earlobe. "Unless, of course, you'd like me to help you."

She shivered, then laughed, deep in her throat, sending tiny tremors through him. The wild ramble over the hills had released more than her tensions. It had unleashed some lingering inhibitions, as well. Something deep inside her responded to his dangerous smile.

"I am feeling a bit tired after my walk, Mr. Donner. I believe I'll take you up on your offer of help."

He stared down at her a moment, caught by surprise, then threw back his head in a roar of laughter. "You're becoming awfully bold. However, I think you've made a very good bargain. Come on." He caught her hand and led her upstairs.

In his room, he stood back, watching her reaction, while she stared about in wonder. Her arms spread out as if to hug the whole scene to her heart.

He had arranged masses of wildflowers in a basket on the white marble table. Another vase of wildflowers stood near the window. The room was ablaze with color and fragrance.

"Oh, Clint." She felt the threat of tears, and swallowed them back. She had been doing entirely too much of this lately.

She turned shining eyes to him.

His voice was a husky caress. "I remember how much you loved the wildflowers that cover these hills in summer. You used to race about the fields, picking them until your arms were overflowing." His tone lowered. "It's a picture of you I'll always carry in my mind."

She moved into his arms, feeling her heart about to explode with the love she felt for him.

"Thank you."

He lifted her chin, and stared deeply into those incredible green eyes, feeling his heart leap. "No, Jordy. Thank *you.*"

He lowered his mouth slowly, loving the way she leaned toward him expectantly. His arms came around her, lifting her, and his mouth crushed hers.

His brother Glen had been wrong all those years ago. He could never get her out of his system. The more he had of her, the more he wanted. She was as essential to him as food. As vital in his life as his music.

"Dinner can wait awhile longer," he muttered thickly. "There are better ways to celebrate an anniversary."

It was another hour before Jordan pulled on a long rose-colored silk dressing gown and matching satin slippers. The color matched the bloom on her cheeks. Clint lounged in the doorway, enjoying the vision.

"Hungry?"

"Starving." She turned to him, and caught his outstretched hand.

As they descended the stairs, he said, "Would you like to make the pasta while I toss the salad?"

"It's comforting to know we can always get a job cooking, if the music business fails," she quipped.

In the kitchen, she stirred her sauce while she waited for the water to boil. Clint handed her a glass of red wine. As she accepted it, he studied her face. The doubt and fears were gone, at least for a little while.

He wanted this night to be perfect. He wanted only to hear her laugh, to see the light dance in her eyes. He wanted only to hold her, to feel her soft and pliant in his arms.

When they carried their dinner to the table, he added another log to the fire, then poured more wine.

Jordan sighed in contentment. If only they could stay here, shut off from the world, lost in the wonder of their feelings.

He tasted the spaghetti. "Wonderful. Jordy, this sauce is superb. You'd better be careful. I may keep you chained to a stove and find myself a new manager."

"You'd never find one as conscientious as the one you have, Mr. Donner."

Her hand rested lightly on the table. Clint's hand moved to cover hers. "I'm aware of that. What did I do before you came into my life, Jordy?"

"I think you managed just fine," she said dryly. Then, with a glint of humor lighting her eyes, she added, "But don't think about getting rid of me just to see if you could go back to managing alone. I'd haunt you."

"I'm sure of that."

She noted his serious look and decided to change the subject. "Do you think you'll be ready for the recording session?"

He nodded. "We'll make it."

The fact was, the songs were almost ready. He had been putting off telling her, stretching out the time spent here with her. He wasn't ready yet to end the idyll.

They ate their fill of pasta and salad, along with crusty garlic bread. When they were finished, Clint took the plates and walked to the kitchen.

"Would you like me to make coffee?" Jordan offered.

"I'll do it. I have something to show you." He hurried away, then returned, carrying a silver goblet.

"What's this?"

He gave her a mysterious smile. "I wanted to surprise you with an exotic dessert." He touched a match to the goblet, and watched her smile of surprise as it flamed.

"Bananas and peaches flambé," he said proudly.

"I'm impressed. If it tastes half as grand as it looks, I'll hire the chef."

It was the perfect ending to a perfect meal. They fed each other bites of the fruit, savoring the sinfully rich brandy sauce. Finally, neither of them could eat another bite.

They cleared the table, then lounged together on a chaise positioned in front of the cozy fire. Clint poured two glasses of red wine. Lovely old ballads played softly on the stereo. Snuggled into the curve of his arm, Jordan rested her cheek against his. Content, they let the firelight and the music wash over them, while the wine eased the tensions of the day.

For long hours into the night, they talked. Never once, Clint noted, did Jordy mention the years of her marriage to Marty. He decided not to press her. Maybe the day would come when she could comfortably tell him all that she had told Danny. Or maybe she would never speak of Marty again. It no longer mattered. For that one brief time today, the floodgates had opened. It had all flowed out of her heart, and he had heard enough to know all he needed to know. Maybe now, he prayed, the past was finally buried for good.

The empty wine bottle rested in a watery ice bucket. The once roaring fire had burned down to gleaming coals. Wrapped in a hazy glow, Clint and Jordan climbed the stairs to bed.

Their lovemaking began slowly, lazily. Too soon it became heated, frenzied. The universe was reduced to this room, this bed, and a passion so intense, it threatened to consume them.

Clint lay quietly, watching her sleep. At last he touched his lips to her eyelids, her cheeks, her lips. Then he slipped silently from the bed. The music played in his brain, demanding to be set down on paper. All evening, the song had been there, fighting for release. There would be no sleep for him this night. But he didn't need sleep now. This woman had given him everything he needed. Her laughter, her tears. But most of all, the music that was her very essence.

The next morning Jordan sat cross-legged in the middle of the bed, braiding her long hair. The night before had been one of the most romantic evenings of her life. The memory of it would carry her through the difficult weeks that loomed ahead. Besides the anticipated piles of correspondence, and endless long distance telephone calls, there was the tension of the recording session awaiting them in Nashville.

For long moments, Clint stood in the doorway, watching her. Did she have any idea how incredibly lovely she was? Dressed in only an ice blue teddy, her slender figure was completely revealed. His gaze trailed over the soft swell of her breasts, then lingered on the faraway look in her eyes. One side of her hair spilled over her shoulder, while she braided the other side. There was an innocence about her that always surprised him. She was an enigma. Despite the fragile beauty, she had great strength of will. Despite all the heartache in her life, she could laugh and be carefree. She was the child of his memories, and the woman who made his pulse quicken. She was the very best thing in his life.

They had discovered something rare and wonderful here at the farm. These few quiet days, away from the frantic pace of their usual routine, had given them both a chance to pause, to breathe deeply. It was easy for love to flourish here in this gentle rural setting.

But what would happen to their love when they returned to Nashville? Would the phones, the fans and the hype drive them apart? His fist clenched by his side.

He leaned a hip against the door, enjoying the vision of Jordy in his bed. He wished he could keep her here forever. This was how he wanted her. His. Exclusively. In his arms when he awoke. At the door when he returned. At his side while he worked.

He reminded himself to be patient. She had been through so much in her young life. She needed time.

Without further thought, he took a step into the room. He had put off this moment as long as he could.

She glanced up, and he watched the smile slowly spread across her face, lighting all her features.

"You're supposed to be working."

He crossed the room and stood, watching as she finished the braid and tied the end. Flipping it behind her shoulder, she knelt in the middle of the bed and held out her arms to him. He kissed her lightly, then backed away.

"I've finished my work."

The statement was so simple, it took her a few moments to understand the implications.

She stopped breathing. "All of it?"

He nodded. "Randy will be up here this afternoon, to start going over the arrangements with me."

She swallowed. "You've completed all the songs?"

Sensing her fears, he forced a lazy smile to reassure her. "Every one of them. We'll have to start rehearsals on these newest ones tomorrow."

"Tomorrow." She slid from the bed and walked to him. Putting her arms around his waist, she pressed her face into his shoulder.

For long moments she was silent. Even her breathing was softer.

Then she pulled away, determined to keep her tone light. "Well, if Randy is coming, I'd better think about fixing something for lunch. Soup and sandwiches, or would you prefer something heartier?"

She pulled on a cotton shirt and stepped into her jeans. "There's corn bread. Or I could bake muffins. I think..."

"Jordy."

"And fruit. Randy loves green apples." She stepped into her shoes.

"Jordy." Clint's voice roughened, breaking into her speech.

She turned.

He smiled gently. "We'll only be a hundred miles from here. We'll record, play our concerts, do the interviews and a few publicity things. It isn't the end of the world."

She returned the smile. "Of course, Clint. I know that."

He watched her as she straightened the quilt on the bed. She glanced up and gave him a smile. It was a little too bright.

He crossed to her. "Jordy. We can make it."

She clung to him for a moment, then pulled away. "I know, Clint. We can make it." She touched her fingers to his lips, then hurried downstairs.

To Jordan, love had always meant one thing. Commitment. But after Marty, she had vowed she would never fall into a trap like that again. She knew now that love was fleeting, intangible. Love was a lot of things, not all of them fairy-tale perfect with happy endings. She had been prepared to live with that knowledge. In fact, she had been prepared to live without ever loving again. But now, with Clint, she wished it could be different. She loved him. It was that simple. But she had already learned the hard way that it was never that simple. Suddenly, she realized she wanted the one thing she most feared—commitment. Or did she?

She wanted to hear Clint pledge his love. Forever. What would love and commitment do to his dreams?

It occurred to her, as it had so often these past days, that he never mentioned marriage.

It was midmorning when Randy arrived, and Jordan answered the door. "Hi, J.D.," he called out as he stood on the porch. A happy grin crinkled the creases of his face, tugging at the corners of his beard.

"Randy. Come on in." Jordan stood aside, closing the door behind him.

"You look great, J.D."

She flushed, aware of his scrutiny.

"I sure was glad to get Clint's call. I couldn't believe it when he said the songs were finished. He must have been up all day and night writing to get this much done."

The sound of music coming from the den stopped abruptly. The door was thrown open, and Clint hurried to grasp his friend's hand.

"That was fast. Did you come by jet?"

Randy laughed. "I practically flew. Are you really ready to record?"

Clint clasped his drummer by the shoulder. "I will be, when you and I finish the arrangements and we get a chance to rehearse with the band. How're they coming with the rest of the songs?"

"Great. We're really tight, Clint. We've never sounded better."

"That's good news." Clint glanced at Jordan, who stood ill at ease, apart from them. "I thought you'd want lunch, before we lock ourselves in the den for the afternoon. Hungry?"

Randy nodded. "You know me. I'm always hungry."

"Everything's ready," Jordan said, avoiding Clint's eyes. "I put your lunch on a tray. That way, you can eat and work in the den at the same time."

They followed her to the kitchen, where Clint lifted a heavy silver tray laden with soup, sandwiches, fruit and cookies. Jordan handed Randy a pot of coffee and two mugs.

"That should keep you for a couple of hours."

When Clint and Randy closed the door to the den, Jordan tidied up the kitchen, then pulled on a jacket and hurried outside.

The den was Clint's private domain. Dominating the room was a concert grand piano. The overhead track lighting was reflected in the ebony gloss of the piano's finish. Along one wall was an open cupboard, containing seven guitars. On the opposite wall were framed copies of all six of Clint's albums, along with the awards he had received, including three gold records and a gold album.

Lovely old French doors opened onto a small, brick-paved courtyard. In warm weather, the open doors allowed the perfume of the roses that ringed the courtyard to drift indoors. As a young bride, Clint's mother had planted roses all around the house and yard. Through the years, they had become a familiar scent, both indoors and out.

Today the doors were closed against the winter chill.

In front of the doors was a desk, covered with sheets of music. Two chairs stood on either side of the desk. Next to this was a long table. Clint set down the heavy tray and pulled up a chair for his friend.

"Dig in."

Randy set down the coffeepot, then turned to study the sheets of music on the desk before meeting Clint's gaze.

"You did it. You really finished all the songs."

Clint grinned.

"And you don't look frazzled. In fact, you don't even look like it was an effort."

Clint shrugged. "When I finally got started, it just rolled."

He poured two cups of coffee, and strolled to the doors. His gaze was arrested by a slender figure striding purposefully across the field.

Randy picked up his coffee mug and stood beside his friend, watching.

Clint's full attention was on the woman. Unknowingly, a warmth came into his eyes. She was heading for the barn, where Clint knew she would spend the next hour or two playing with Mollie's puppies.

Randy watched until she disappeared below a ridge. Then he turned to study the radiant glow on his friend's face. "Being at the farm certainly agrees with you."

Clint looked up with a slow smile. "Umm. I think I've discovered magic in this country air."

"The lady certainly is magic. You look better then I've seen you look in years." He slapped Clint on the back. "Come on. We've got work to do."

Hours later both men were so engrossed in their music that neither of them even glanced up at the soft tap on the door.

Jordan waited, knocked a second time, then pushed open the door to the den.

Two heads were bent over the desk, writing furiously.

"I made dinner."

Jordan watched as Clint handed a sheet of music to Randy, added some notations, then handed a second page over. Randy nodded, made a few changes, then handed them back.

"Would you two care to take a break now?"

Clint looked up. "What, Jordy?"

"I said, would you like some dinner?"

His expression was completely blank.

She walked closer. "Food. You know—a loaf of bread, a jug of wine."

He gave her a lopsided grin. Her heart tilted.

"I'm not hungry. How about you, Randy?"

"I'm always hungry." The drummer patted his ample waist.

"Want to take a break?"

Randy shook his head. "I'd rather eat while I work. Would you mind, J.D.?"

She smiled knowingly. "No. I expected as much when I didn't see either of you all afternoon. How's it going?"

"Great." Clint growled the word, then rubbed the back of his neck tiredly. "We should be done in a few hours."

"Why don't you both come in the kitchen and fill your plates. I'll bring the coffee and dessert in here."

"You don't mind?" Clint ran his fingers along her cheek. He wanted to hold her, but he understood her caution at displaying any emotion in front of Randy.

"No. I expected you to work right through the night."

Randy pushed back his chair and started through the doorway.

Clint caught Jordan's arm and held her back. Touching her hair, he murmured, "I'll try to finish before bedtime."

"It's okay, Clint. I don't mind."

"I do." He could hardly wait until tonight to hold her again. He had learned to love their shared intimacy. He needed it, especially tonight.

Chapter Eleven

Clint snapped on the lamp on the night table. Soft light illuminated the figure in the bed. While he unbuttoned his shirt, he studied the cascade of her dark hair, a stark contrast to the white pillow.

She had loosened the braids, leaving a mass of crimped curls and frizz, which added to her wild, Gypsy appearance. Long dark eyelashes cast jagged shadows on her high cheekbones.

He undressed quickly, eager to feel her in his arms. As he settled beside her, she stirred, but didn't wake completely. He reached over, snapped off the light and drew her against him.

"I missed you." He ran his lips across her cheek and upward to her temple.

She sighed, and dropped a hand on his arm. "What time is it?" He loved the breathless quality of her voice when she was barely awake.

"Nearly three o'clock."

She stirred. "In the morning?"

"No. Afternoon." His tone was too tender to be sarcastic. She didn't take the bait.

He dropped light kisses on her raised eyebrows.

"Where's Randy?"

"Here in bed. He's on the other side of you."

She sat bolt upright.

Clint chuckled, low in his throat. "That's one way to get your attention."

"Oh, you tease!" She lay back down, but not before feeling around the bed with her hand, just to be certain. "Where is Randy sleeping?"

"In your old room. Do you mind?"

"Of course not. As long as he's not in bed with us, I don't mind where he sleeps."

"Jordy."

"Umm." She snuggled into his arms.

"You've been distant all day. Why?" He thought he knew the answer, but he wanted her to talk about it.

"I wasn't distant. You were just busy."

"Jordy." Seeing her closed eyes, he leaned over her on one elbow. "Is it Randy?"

Her eyelids fluttered. She met his gaze, then closed her eyes against the question.

"Does it bother you that he knows about us?" He twined a strand of dark hair around his finger, then tugged it when she remained silent.

She opened her eyes. "Yes. I'm uncomfortable about it." She licked her lips. "The guys in the band are close, as close as family. If one of them knows, all of them will eventually know about us."

"So what?"

What she and Clint had discovered was too precious to share with anyone. At least not yet. But she couldn't find the words to tell him.

"I'm their manager, Clint. I'm not sure I can function as well if the word gets out that I'm..."

He heard the anguish in her voice, the reluctance to even say the words aloud. "Are you saying you won't stay with me when we get back to Nashville?"

"You mean in your... friend's mausoleum in Belle Meade?"

He smiled. "She's home from her tour. So I'll go back to my apartment in the Belle Meade Club. It's big and comfortable. You'll like it, Jordy."

She took a deep breath. "I think it would be better if we each stayed in our own apartment."

"But I..."

"I don't think either of us would like the kind of gossip we'd be reading if this were to become public knowledge." She placed a hand over his lips. "You know I'm right, Clint."

He expelled an angry breath. No. He wasn't at all certain she was right. He'd never knowingly expose her to gossip and rumors. But he wasn't sure he could calmly let her go, now that he had tasted her love. He wanted her with him. Needed her.

"Will you think about moving into my place?"

"I've thought about it. The answer is no."

His lips began nuzzling her throat. "Maybe I can persuade you."

She felt the warmth of his lips on her skin, and the familiar sensation that began curling deep inside her. "I'm willing to let you try. I'm easy."

He groaned against her collarbone. "I wish you were. You're the toughest one hundred pounds of steel I've ever met."

With that, his lips closed over hers in a kiss that was at once loving and harsh.

She sensed a new urgency to his lovemaking. Always before, he had tempered his passion with gentleness, as if aware of his superior size and strength. Now he abandoned all caution. In one swift motion, he stripped the delicate teddy from her. His hands and lips moved over her in an almost desperate frenzy, needing to feel her response match his driving needs.

She tasted the hunger in his kiss. He seemed to have an almost obsessive desire to possess her, to prove that she needed him as much as he needed her.

In her drowsy state, she was quickly aroused. She thought by now she knew everything about his lovemaking. But tonight, everything was new. He ran a tongue between her breasts, then slowly circled each one before taking a nipple between his teeth lightly. He continued teasing her breast while she writhed and moaned her desire. His lips roamed her body, bringing her higher, until she thought she would explode from wanting him.

"Tell me you want me." His lips crushed hers. The words were murmured inside her mouth.

"I do. I do, Clint."

"Tell me how much you need me, Jordy."

But she didn't think she could speak. She felt the shuddering need cutting off her breath.

"Tell me, Jordy." His voice was a low, throaty growl against her mouth.

"I need you. Oh Clint, I need you." It was a plaintive cry against his lips.

He took her, as desperately as he had the first time, feeling wave after wave shudder through her. And when she thought she could give no more, he led her even higher, quickly taking her beyond all thought.

For a long while, she lay locked in his arms, her face pressed tightly to his shoulder. His face rested in her hair, and he inhaled the scent of her perfume. It was a delicate wildflower fragrance that would always remind him of her. She was a wildflower who was finally struggling to grow free and blossom into a thing of beauty. If he tried to pluck her, or plant her in his garden, would she lose the very qualities that made her special?

Clint rolled to his side, then drew her firmly into his arms. She pressed her lips to his throat. He ran one hand up her cheek, then wiped the sheen from her forehead and temple.

She wrapped her arms about his waist, and fitted herself perfectly to him. Her breathing softened as she grew sleepy.

He ran a hand through the tangled strands of hair that spilled about her neck and shoulders. He felt a fierce protectiveness toward her. He wanted to keep her here with him, away from the world. Yet they both had other lives to lead, careers that pulled at them.

They had to face the world beyond this farm. They had to find a way to survive in that other world.

"I love you, Jordy." His lips nuzzled her ear.

Her breath was warm against his throat. He leaned over to study her. She was asleep.

More gently now, he stroked the silken skin of her back and drew her closer. Then, pulling the blanket around them, he listened to the steady beating of her heart as it lulled him to join her in sleep.

"Want me to help with the dishes, J.D.?"

"No thanks, Randy. You and Clint have enough on your minds with all that music to pack up. When are you calling for the first rehearsal?"

"This afternoon. Around four. That'll give us time to drive back to Nashville and run off copies of the music for all the guys." He deposited his dishes on the counter. "Good breakfast. Thanks, J.D."

She smiled. "You're lucky. Breakfast is one of the few meals I can't ruin."

"Hey. Quit being silly. I thought it was great. You can cook breakfast in my kitchen anytime."

Clint smiled at their easy banter. This morning, Jordan seemed more relaxed in Randy's presence. He began to nurture the secret hope that she would reconsider her decision to stay at her own apartment when they returned to Nashville.

They had found no time for quiet talk this morning. There had been only a hurried kiss before they showered and dressed. Now it was time to pack up the cars, and close up the house.

He watched her as she busied herself in his bright, airy kitchen. She looked so natural here. This cozy room was a secure retreat from the harsh realities of her world. Yet she seemed resigned to going back.

They couldn't even drive back to Nashville together. Clint had his car and Jordan had driven up in hers. He pushed aside the vaguely unsettling feelings. They would have to snatch some time together later. Right now, there were too many details demanding his attention.

Jordan stood out of view, in the shadows, and watched Clint. His eyes were fixed on a distant spot on the ceiling. His clenched hands stretched out before him as he drew the note out to its fullest.

When the song ended, there was complete silence for several seconds. Then a technician's voice could be heard from the sound booth.

"Great, Clint. Ready for a playback?"

He nodded, and bowed his head, intent on every note that flowed through the speakers.

To Jordan's ear, the number had been performed flawlessly. She saw Clint's head come up sharply.

"Hold it there, Steve."

There was an abrupt silence throughout the studio. "Give me that playback, up to that point again."

Once more, Clint adopted that air of deep concentration. Jordan watched as he tensed, waiting for the offending note. He raised a hand toward the booth.

"That's it. Right there. I want to go over that part again." He was already putting on the headphones.

Into the microphone, he instructed the engineers, "Let's do another vocal. I want it tighter."

This had been going on for days. And nights. The band had laid down the first tracks, playing only the instrumental parts of the songs. Then Clint and the backup singers had joined the band for some of the vocals. The six regular members of the band had been enlarged to include a mandolin, fiddle, saxophone and synthesizer. Added to that were the regular backup singers, plus three studio singers. With that many talented people, there was bound to be some friction. Yet the sessions were going surprisingly smoothly.

They recorded, as so many country and western musicians did, using the open sound that was typical of Nashville recordings. The involvement of all the musicians and singers together during the session gave the record a more spontaneous sound, which musicians the world over recognized as the "Nashville sound."

The studio they used was one of the newer buildings along Music Row. Years ago, Clint's first record had been made in one of the old converted houses that doubled as a recording studio. Now, they were under contract to a major label, which had built a glass-and-stone tower that dwarfed the other buildings on the block.

This area was a reminder of the simplicity of the fledgling dream of country music, and the complex industry it spawned.

Randy's long hours had paid off. He had rehearsed the band until they were nearly perfect. Jordan had never heard Clint sound better. The music that had poured from him at the farm came straight from his heart. And it showed in these recordings.

Her own days were too full to spend much time at the studio. Now that Clint was recording, she was gearing up for the onslaught of public appearances that inevitably followed. Jordan sighed and slipped unseen from the studio.

By the time this album was released across the country, Clint would be spending nearly all his time on the road. Jordan was determined to garner as much publicity for him on this tour as possible.

Back at her office, she settled behind her desk and sifted through the mountain of mail. It would be evening before she would even make a dent in this. She had to make some long-distance calls to the West Coast, but they had to be attended to later, because of the time difference. She realized with a little groan that she should have taken time to eat lunch instead of going to the recording studio. But Clint had asked her to stop by to talk, if only for a few minutes. They hadn't had a moment alone in days. It was only after she got there that she realized that he was so caught up in the recording, he had completely forgotten about her.

She poured a cup of strong coffee. This would have to do.

"I hoped I'd find you here."

Jordan's head twisted at the familiar voice. Clint paused in the doorway, his gaze moving from the mound of correspondence on her desk to her face.

He closed the door and moved across the room. "I phoned your apartment." He smiled gently. "Figured you'd still be working. Don't you know it's nearly ten o'clock?''

"It can't be helped. These people just won't stop pestering you with bills and requests for appearances."

His hands gripped her arms, lifting her from the chair. As she opened her mouth to protest, his lips covered hers.

They stood for long moments, letting the warmth of the kiss flow over them.

"Umm. I needed that." Clint buried his lips in a tangle of hair. "Come and have dinner with me."

"I can't. The bills . . ."

"Burn them." His hands roamed her face, brushing away a strand of hair, tracing the outline of her lips.

"All right. You're the boss. Should I burn the requests for appearances, too?"

He studied her eyes, a glint of laughter shimmering in his. "No, I have to draw the line somewhere. Answer those."

She grinned and drew him closer.

Clint felt more lighthearted than he had in days, just being with her.

"Come on, Jordy. I know a wonderful little Italian restaurant."

She began to shake her head. "I can't."

"I'll ply you with wine."

"Uh-huh. I know what you're up to."

"I'll play the concertina. I'll even sing Italian arias."

"That does it. How can I refuse my one and only chance to hear the great Clint Donner sing opera?" She grabbed her coat and caught his hand. "But I still think this is a terrible way to run an office."

"We'll talk about it over pasta."

They drove in silence, with only the car radio playing in the background. The lights of Nashville were a colorful backdrop against the night sky. They parked, and walked among the throngs of tourists to Printer's Alley.

The restaurant was small and intimate. Inside, the ceiling was arched like a cathedral, with the arches repeated in the doorways, and on the aged brick walls. The intimate booths were constructed of old barn wood, and shaped like church pews. Candles flickered on tables and in sconces on the walls. In a back room, someone was playing a mandolin.

They were led to a corner booth, where Clint ordered a bottle of red wine.

"All right. I'll allow you to ply me with wine." Jordan sipped her drink, then studied Clint's face. "Are you pleased with the way the recording session is going?"

"Yes. So far, no major problems."

She noted the shadows beneath his eyes. "But...?"

He looked puzzled. "But what?"

"You tell me, Clint. No problems, but something's bothering you."

He frowned. "Jordy, I..."

He stopped abruptly, as the waiter brought their salads. When they were alone, he ate in silence.

Jordan was puzzled. A little while ago, he had seemed happy, carefree. Now he seemed tense, edgy. She glanced at his face in the candlelight. The angles and planes seemed more pronounced. The firmly clenched jaw, the little pulse that throbbed at his temple, were indications that he was fighting for control.

He leaned back, sipping his wine, determined to relax. "I haven't seen you in days. How've you been?"

"Fine." She smiled as the waiter removed their salad plates. "Working hard. There were a lot of wrinkles to smooth out when I got back to the office."

"I thought I asked you to stop by the studio while we were recording."

Jordan thought she detected an underlying note of accusation in his tone. "I did. Several times. But you were always busy recording. I didn't want to disturb you, so I just watched and listened for a while, then left without a word."

"I see." He thought he had only imagined her perfume in the studio. At least now he knew he wasn't going mad.

His tension seemed to ease a little.

The waiter brought two plates mounded with pasta. With a grin, Jordan and Clint dug into their dinner.

"Oh. That was wonderful," Jordan sighed some time later as she sat back, replete.

"Umm. I think I forgot to eat today. Too busy with the album."

Two strolling musicians approached their booth, smiling broadly. One played the mandolin. The other had a concertina.

"Does the lady have a request?"

A gleam of impish humor sparkled in Jordan's eyes. "Yes. I do." She turned to Clint, then said, "I'd love to hear an aria. My escort claims he can play the concertina and can sing in a perfectly marvelous Italian tenor."

Clint shook his head at the looks of surprise on the musicians' faces, then burst out laughing. "I did promise, didn't I?"

She nodded her head. "Yes you did. And I expect you to keep your part of the bargain."

"How about one out of two?"

"Meaning?"

"Meaning, I'll sing, if you'll let me off the hook on the concertina. I'd rather let the expert play."

"All right. Do your Irish tenor impression." Jordan was trying not to laugh. This was serious business.

Clint asked the musicians if they knew the music to *Pagliacci*. They beamed and played the opening strains of the classic aria.

Clint took Jordan's hand, and began singing to her, softly at first, then allowing his voice to swell with the music. Though his voice was far from being a tenor, he managed the notes admirably.

The murmur of voices in the room gradually stopped. Waiters paused in their work, watching, listening, nodding their approval. And though it started out to be a joke, Clint felt Jordan's tremor as the music grew more serious. The beauty of the lyrics washed over her, as he sang the haunting lament of the cheating spouse and unrequited love. She struggled to remain composed. Her gaze lowered to study the linen tablecloth.

When the song ended, the musicians applauded Clint's efforts. All around them, people stood and applauded, smiling their approval. The musicians bowed deeply to Jordan and Clint, before moving on to entertain the occupants of another table.

For long moments they were silent. Clint touched Jordan's hand. "I'm sorry it was so sad. Has it made you unhappy?"

She smiled tenderly. "After I got past the hurting part, I enjoyed it. In any language, love can be wonderful—and terrible."

He saw the flash of sadness before she blinked it away.

Her smile grew. "You know so much, Clint. Poetry, opera." She glanced away, embarrassed. "Sometimes, I feel so inadequate."

"You, Jordy?" The look he gave her was filled with tenderness. "You fill my life."

The waiter returned with a pastry cart, and Jordan studied the selections carefully, glad for the distraction. Everything on the cart looked inviting. Finally she settled on a *canolli,* the wonderful Italian pastry filled with cream and sprinkled with nuts and powdered sugar.

"Oh, Clint. You have to taste this. It's wonderful."

Relieved to see her smile again, he opened his mouth, and she offered him a taste. The look on his face told her how much he enjoyed it.

"Umm. One more bite."

She laughed, and offered him a second taste. When she finished the rest, he reached over and dabbed at the corner of her mouth. Then he leaned closer, and brushed his lips over hers. They tasted of wine and powdered sugar.

His gaze rested a moment on her lips. Abruptly he touched her face. His voice was thick with emotion. "Come on, Jordy. Let's get out of here."

When he started the car, he turned to her in the darkness. "Would you be willing to come to my place?"

She shook her head. "No. I'd like to go home."

He seemed about to say something, then changed his mind. Putting the car in gear, he flicked on the radio.

At Jordan's apartment, he held out his hand for the key. After opening the door, he followed her inside. The moment the door was closed, he drew her into his embrace. The kiss was warm, firm, possessive. For one fleeting moment, she hesitated. Then she melted into his arms, loving the feel of his lips on hers.

"Oh, God, Jordy. It's been too long." His lips moved against her ear, sending a rush of heat along her spine.

"I've tried to see you," she murmured against his jaw. "But there are so many people around you. There's just never any time alone."

His tongue flicked her ear, causing shivers to go through her. "And I've called you at the office, only to get that damned answering device. Sometimes, during the day, I just want to hear your voice. Just for a few minutes."

His mouth found the sensitive little hollow of her throat, and began nibbling. She arched her neck, loving the delicious tingles his touch caused.

His lips moved lower, probing beneath the neckline of her shirt for the soft swell of breast. "All these clothes," he growled, as his hands came up to the buttons of her blouse.

She slipped out of her coat, and felt the blouse fall away from her shoulders. In one swift motion, he slid the narrow straps of her teddy down her arms and watched as it drifted down about her waist.

Her fingers fumbled with the buttons of his shirt, wanting to feel the warmth of his skin, but he drew her closer, blocking her attempts. His hands, his lips, began working their magic, heating her flesh. His lips kept coming back to hers. He needed to taste her, to reassure himself that she was here in his arms, that this wasn't a dream.

A ringing telephone shattered the silence of the room.

"Oh, no." Clint lifted his head. Smoldering dark eyes stared into green luminous pools that were glazed with passion. "Do you have to answer that?"

She took a deep breath, trying to shake the feelings that clouded her thinking. "I...yes, I think I should."

He started to let her go, then suddenly drew her closer, kissing her firmly. "Thirty seconds. No more. Whoever it is, get rid of them."

She smiled, then walked across the room and picked up the receiver.

"Yes? Oh, hello, Randy." Her gaze met Clint's across the room. "Yes, he's here."

Clint scowled. As he took the phone from Jordan's hand, he caught her, holding her against him while he spoke.

"Yes, Randy. What is it?" His hand stroked her back. As Randy's voice hummed through the phone, he lowered the receiver and lifted her face for a lingering kiss.

"Okay. We'll work on it in the morning." He ran a hand through the dark silk of her hair, and pressed her closer.

He listened for a moment longer, then swore. "You'd better be right." His tone became more clipped. "All right. Fifteen minutes. I'll be there."

He dropped the receiver, leaving it dangling off the hook. His arms came around her, and his fingertips caressed the satin skin of her back.

His voice thickened. "I have to go, Jordy. Randy's meeting me at my place in a few minutes. He has some important changes in the arrangement of one of the songs we're recording tomorrow."

He kissed her deeply, torn between the demands of his work and the need to give in to the passion that flared between them.

"Come with me." He spoke the words against her lips.

"No, Clint."

"Then let me come back here when we're finished."

"I know you two well enough to know that once you get started, you'll work through the entire night."

"I'll call you."

"No." She took a deep breath. "The office is in a shambles. I'll be on the phone for hours tomorrow. I need to get there early." She saw the frustration in his eyes. "I'm sorry."

"Not half as sorry as I am. We can't keep this up, Jordy."

"I don't see any choice." With as much dignity as she could muster, she pulled up the straps of her teddy, and walked to where her shirt had dropped.

"Will I see you tomorrow?" He waited, with his hand on the knob.

She shrugged. "I don't know, Clint. We can try."

He strode across the room and took her in his arms. The kiss he gave her left her breathless. "No matter what, I intend to see you tomorrow. Even if I have to leave half the population of Nashville cooling their heels."

When the door closed, she sat down weakly on the edge of the bed. Welcome back, she thought angrily.

The reality of the crazy world they lived in was closing in on her.

Chapter Twelve

Jordan unlocked the office door and picked up the pile of mail that had been delivered while she was out to lunch. It had been one of those uncomfortable business luncheons, with the producer of a local talk show pressing for Clint's appearance before he left on tour. Jordan had tried to explain how tight their schedule was, especially since Clint was still in the process of recording the final cuts of the album.

She knew Clint's loyalty to the people of this town. She didn't need the constant reminders that Bill Lawrence, the producer, kept throwing at her.

"Should I remind you, Ms. Hunter, who Clint's first real fans were?"

She remained adamant.

"How about it, J.D.?" he pressed a few minutes later. "Why couldn't Clint just give us an hour or two in the next week? His hometown fans love him."

At her insistent refusal, he coaxed, "Would you at least agree to bring Clint around to the studio for just one small segment of the show?"

She tried to explain that recording an album was an all-consuming job. It wasn't just the hours spent in the studio. It was the emotional drain of sweating over every single note, and every tiny detail.

In the end, she had agreed to phone the producer's secretary by early next week if there was any chance Clint could appear on the show.

As she sifted through the mail, Jordan switched on the phone answering device. Her efforts were beginning to pay off. There were two requests in the mail for interviews, one with a nationally prominent newsmagazine. She paused to listen to the next phone message. This call was from a promoter in the West who had heard that Clint would be touring California within the next few months. If she would fly out to meet with him, he would make it worth Clint's while.

Suddenly there was a muttered oath on the machine, followed by a deep, familiar voice.

"Damn it, Jordy. Do you know how long it's been?"

She dropped the mail and turned up the volume on the machine.

"I have to see you soon, or I'll go crazy. Do you think you could drop by the recording studio sometime today? I'll be there until ten or so." His voice grew firmer. "No matter when you show up, I'll drop

everything so we can spend some time together."
There was a slight pause. She could hear the laughter
in his voice. "I guess that's all I'll say in case you have
visitors in the office."

She pressed the rewind button, heard the jumble of
squeaking voices, then stopped and replayed his message several times.

Deep in thought, she smiled and leaned back in the
chair, staring at the passing stream of pedestrians and
traffic. It had been too long. Every night, when she
returned to her apartment, the walls seemed to close
in on her. The loneliness was even more intolerable
since she'd returned from the farm. She had begun
playing her stereo morning and night for company and
to keep from thinking about Clint. She jumped every
time the phone rang.

She had never felt so alive as she had during those
wonderful days with Clint. He made her laugh, he
challenged her mind, he teased and even fought with
her. She shivered slightly. And when he loved her, she
felt there was nothing they couldn't do together.

She made up her mind quickly. No matter how
much work piled up, tonight belonged to Clint.

Jordan left the office in a rush. She had wanted to
look cool and collected when she saw Clint. But, as
usual, the phone calls kept coming, and before she
knew it, she had glanced at her watch in alarm. Ten
o'clock. She had planned to surprise Clint by showing up at the recording studio in plenty of time to hear
the band's latest cut. Now, she would be lucky just to
catch him before he left for the night. She gasped as a

sudden thought struck. She hadn't phoned to let him know she was coming. What if she missed him?

It had been days since she had last seen Clint, and then it had been only to get his signature on some documents. Being that close to him without being able to touch him was a torment. It had been a painful reminder of what they had shared.

She pressed the accelerator harder. She never realized there were so many traffic lights between the office and the recording studio.

Bringing the car to a screeching halt at the curb, Jordan grabbed her keys and raced up the steps to the front door. She pulled on the handle, then stepped back. It was locked. Peering through the grill, she saw lights at the rear of the building. With a sigh, she flew down the steps and made her way to the far side of the studio.

Clint glanced at his watch for the hundredth time. It was nearly ten fifteen. And still no sign of Jordy. He hadn't heard a word from her. If she wasn't coming, the least she could have done was to call the studio and leave word with one of the technicians. He had called an end to the session half an hour ago. Everyone had gone home.

He swore in frustration. Why had he counted on her?

He packed up the last sheets of music and stuffed them into his briefcase. With angry, jerking movements, he pulled on his jacket and walked to the door.

When he pulled it open, he collided with soft curves.

"Oh, Clint. I'm so glad you haven't left yet." One of the studio singers stood just outside the door.

He looked beyond her to the parking lot. Besides his car and one other, it was completely empty.

"What's wrong?" He pulled the door shut behind him.

"My car won't start. The battery's dead, I guess. Can I hitch a ride?"

"Sure." He picked up the briefcase and led the way to his car.

As he opened the door, the interior light flashed on, bathing both of them in amber light. He glanced down at the woman beside him. Her lips were parted in a smile that spoke of invitation.

Her hair was soft and blond, her eyes pale blue. He felt a flash of annoyance.

As she settled herself in his car, she touched his arm. "Thanks, Clint. I really appreciate this."

He closed the door, walked to the driver's side and climbed in.

Her perfume was heavy, sweet. It filled the car. He started the engine, then pressed a button to lower the window. "Where can I drop you?"

"It's on the other side of town. I'll show you."

She glanced across at him, lowering her lashes. "You sounded terrific tonight, Clint."

"Thanks." He flipped on the radio, then turned up the volume, wanting to blot out her voice. It was the wrong pitch. Even with the window open, her perfume was cloying. She didn't smell like wildflowers. Her hair wasn't dark and wild. Her eyes weren't green.

He turned to her before slipping the car into gear. "Your name is . . . Chris, isn't it?"

She nodded.

"I'm feeling really drained, Chris. I hope you don't mind if I forego the small talk. I'd like to just listen to the radio and drive."

In the darkness, his brooding eyes seemed even darker and more mysterious. The slight frown made his handsome face more fascinating.

She reached over to touch his sleeve. "Hey, I don't mind at all."

He turned the radio even louder, then swung from the parking lot.

"How about that, Clint? They're playing your song. What a coincidence." The trill of feminine laughter filtered through the open window as the car pulled away.

Jordan stood in the shadow of the building, unable to move. She watched in frozen horror as Clint and the blonde emerged from the lights of the recording studio and walked together to the darkened parking lot.

Her hands clenched at her sides as the woman smiled up into Clint's lowered face. Something deep inside her knotted when the woman's hand touched Clint's arm. And when his car pulled away with a screech of tires, Jordan's hand flew to her mouth at the sound of the blaring music and the woman's lilting laughter. She felt as if she would suffocate. She couldn't breathe. It was all happening again.

* * *

How long had she been driving? She didn't even remember turning down this street. Jordan glanced up to see the neon lights of Will's diner. As she opened the door, the old man looked up in surprise.

"Jordan Hunter. Don't you know you shouldn't be out alone at night?"

Seeing her expression, he set down the newspaper he had been reading, and poured her a cup of coffee.

"Here. You look like you could use this."

She wrapped her hands around the mug. "Thanks, Will. I sure could."

"Something wrong, Jordan?"

She stared into her coffee, avoiding his eyes. "It's been a long day. Sometimes I feel like it's been one long, hard grind."

He stared at her bowed head, lowered in defeat. "Things will look better in the morning." He poured himself a mug of steaming coffee, and blew into it before taking a gulp. "I've lived three times as long as you. And there's one thing I've found."

She glanced up.

"Some people fall apart, even if they just stub a toe. You can spot 'em. Always crying how life isn't fair. And some people—" he stared pointedly at Jordan "—just take everything life dishes out, and keep on getting back up to try again." He gave her a wink. "You're no quitter, Jordan. You know the sun will shine again, no matter how many clouds there are now."

She offered him a weak smile. "Thanks, Will. I owe you one."

"Now. How about a bowl of soup?"

"No thanks." She wouldn't be able to eat a thing. Her stomach was tied up in knots.

She finished the coffee in three gulps and dropped some change on the counter. "Thanks, Will. I think what I need is some sleep. Good night."

His eyes followed her slender form as she walked stiffly from the diner. She was one fine lady. A pretty little thing like that shouldn't be out all alone in the night. Fact is, she shouldn't ever have to be alone at all.

The phone was ringing as Jordan unlocked the door to her apartment. She ignored it.

Stripping off her clothes, she stepped under the shower and felt the stinging spray begin to infuse warmth back into her cold body.

She put on her oversize football jersey and climbed beneath the covers. Pulling the blanket over her head, she lay very still, listening to the ticking of the clock on her bedside table.

We aren't married. We've made no commitment. I have no hold on Clint. And I have no right to expect him to be faithful.

She rolled to her other side, and balled her hands into fists.

What did I expect? He's a celebrity. There are a lot of women who fantasize about him. Given the opportunity, they'd grab the chance to be with him. An hour, an evening, a weekend.

How could she blame them? Aren't you guilty of the same thing? her mind taunted.

One week. The words drummed in her brain. Seven days with Clint. One short week. Not exactly grounds for love and marriage.

She had gone to him with her eyes wide open. She had agreed to stay with him for as long as he wanted. And those glorious days at the farm had been much more than she had ever hoped for. She had glimpsed heaven.

And now? She felt a terrible rage building inside her. All those good intentions, to be nothing more to Clint Donner than his manager, the best manager in the business. All her promises to herself, to learn from her past mistake, to remain aloof from romantic entanglements. They had all flown out the window. All he'd had to do was crook his finger and she had gone flying to him like a love-struck teenager.

He had probably known from the beginning that he would have her in his own good time. And she had made it so easy for him. She had certainly destroyed her credibility as a dispassionate business woman.

The tears began, at first burning her throat as she tried to swallow them back, and then flowing freely, until the bed shook with her sobs. Long into the night she cried, until, drained, exhausted, she washed her face and turned out the lights.

When the tears subsided, they were replaced by a burning, simmering anger. When was she ever going to learn? How many times did she have to have her heart broken before she found a way to keep it intact?

She closed her eyes, swallowing the bitter bile of fury that was lodged in her throat. Maybe there was something about a one-man woman that brought out the worst in men. Maybe once a man knew she was his, for as long as he wanted, he no longer wanted her at all. Maybe a restless man like Clint always needed a fresh challenge. He had to keep tempting fate, to leave the familiar behind in search of the new, the untraveled path. Hadn't he turned his back on the home of his youth in search of his dreams? Only a fool would hang around until he grew tired of his wandering.

She hovered on the edges of sleep. Clint's face swam before her, smiling tenderly, then laughing. His laughter was joined by the trill of a woman's voice. But he was no longer Clint. The face that slowly came into focus belonged to a bleary-eyed Marty. How many times had she covered up his drinking, doing his job as well as her own? Jordan was staring down at a bed, her bed, hers and Marty's, seeing Marty and the very young blonde in his arms, staring up at her. Flushed and embarrassed at being caught in such a humiliating situation, the blonde had turned to Marty. And he had burst into drunken laughter. A moment later, the blonde joined him in nervous giggles. That was the moment Jordan had been pushed over the edge. In that instant, Jordan had known what she had to do. She knew she had to leave Marty, for the sake of her sanity, while she still had some dignity. Except that he left first, on business, and never came back. The official report was death due to an auto accident. There had been no other car involved. He had missed a turn in the highway. The once beautiful young woman beside him was unrecognizable when pulled from the mangled remains.

Jordan awoke in the darkness, screaming. Her pillow was bathed in sweat.

For the rest of the night, she lay awake, trembling.

Clint's voice on the telephone was a shout. "What do you mean you're flying to L.A.?"

"Just what I said. You've had a terrific offer to do a top-rated T.V. show while you're there. I'm flying out to start the preliminary discussions with the show's producer."

His words were clipped. "When do you leave?"

"My plane leaves at three."

"I'm coming over, Jordy."

"No." She licked her lips. "I've...got some errands to run before I go to the airport. I was just going out the door when you called."

"Then I'll drive you."

"There's no need..."

"I said I'll be there. See that you wait."

He slammed down the receiver and went to find his drummer.

"Randy, I have to leave for an hour."

"But..."

"Something important's come up. Call a lunch break. Or run through the songs a couple of times. I don't care what you do. I'm going."

Randy tapped his fingers nervously on a music stand and watched his friend disappear through the doorway. He should have known things were going along too smoothly. The sudden tension in Clint the past few days was becoming contagious. Everyone was beginning to feel edgy.

Clint drove at top speed. She wasn't going to get away with this. What was eating at her?

For days he had listened to that infuriating machine answer her phone at the office. And no matter what time he called her apartment, there was no answer. She was definitely avoiding him, but he couldn't figure out why.

He pulled up in front of the office and unconsciously squared his shoulders. She wasn't leaving until they'd had this out.

When he opened the door, she looked up from her desk.

"My luggage is over there."

He didn't even glance where she pointed. "I'll get it in a minute."

He stopped at her desk and planted his feet wide. "How about starting with, 'Hello, Clint. It's good to see you'?"

Her eyes widened for an instant. Then, with absolutely no inflection in her voice, she intoned, "Hello, Clint. It's good to see you."

"Is it?"

"Yes." She sighed and forced a brightness she didn't feel. "And thank you for offering to drive me. Although I really could have managed alone."

"I'm sure you could." He studied her. His voice softened. "It really is good to see you, Jordy. What's been taking up all your time?"

"You."

He blinked.

"Actually, your career. The phone's been ringing off the hook." She held up a stack of correspondence. "At least half of this mail is made up of requests for you to do a concert or a benefit or a show."

His gaze never left her face. His voice lowered. "You never returned *my* calls."

She avoided his eyes and stood quickly. "I meant to. But I've been tied up." She glanced at her watch. "We'd better leave if I'm going to stop at my apartment before I go to the airport."

As she bent to her luggage, he studied the tailored business suit she wore, and found himself wondering if she was wearing that sexy bit of silk and lace beneath. What did she call it? A hint of a smile touched the corners of his lips. A teddy. He fought the urge to hold her.

He caught her arm and was surprised to feel her flinch. "Do we have a minute to talk, Jordy?"

She stared into his eyes for a moment, then looked quickly away. "No. I'll miss my plane." She stepped back. "Let's just talk on the way."

"All right." He bent to lift her bulging suitcase. "Planning on staying a while?"

"This could drag on. I thought I'd be prepared for a few days or a week."

She picked up a makeup case and followed him to the car.

As he started the ignition, he asked, "What do you need to do at the apartment?"

"I want to pick up a file I left there." She shrugged. "Turn down the heat, plug in a light timer. That's about all. Luckily, there's no pet to worry about. Or worse," she added, "a husband or children to fuss over."

He lit a cigarette. "No ties to bind you. Is that how you like it, Jordy?"

A knife sliced through her heart. "Absolutely." She turned to stare out the window.

He watched her stiff profile, wondering how to break through the wall she had built.

As he pulled up to her apartment, she hurried from the car before he could step out. "I'll just be a minute."

It was obvious that she didn't want him coming up with her. He sat and watched the smoke from his cigarette curl out the vent. It was just as obvious that something had happened to revive old hurts. The past wasn't buried after all.

She was inside for a long time. She emerged clutching a file folder. "All right. We're just going to make it."

He crushed out the cigarette, put the car in gear and headed toward the airport. Clint found himself wondering if she had deliberately delayed inside to avoid having to talk to him.

"Did you get my message to come to the studio?" He turned to glance at her.

For a moment her hands went still. Then she busied herself stuffing the file folder into her briefcase. Her mind whirled.

Tell him the truth. Tell him you saw him. Tell him you know what he does on the nights he doesn't see you. She lifted her chin. She couldn't speak the truth without breaking down. Dignity. If she couldn't have Clint, she could at least have some self-respect. She would not resort to ugly scenes and shouted accusations and—a flood of tears. She had promised herself she would never again be reduced to hysteria over a man.

"I don't know. I might have. I've had so many messages."

She studied the massive chunks of rock along the highway. Layers of silver, bronze and ochre ledgerock framed the roads and parkways.

"It was five days ago, Jordy. I waited for you. I expected to hear from you if you couldn't make it. And I've had no messages from you since." His hands gripped the wheel tightly. "Why?"

She was relieved to see the entrance to the Nashville Metropolitan Airport. Taking a deep breath, she turned to face him. "I told you. I've been busy. Here's my terminal. You don't have to go in with me. Just let me out here."

As the car drew up to the curb, she hurried out. Clint opened the trunk and lifted her suitcase. She signaled a porter, then turned to Clint.

"Thanks again. I'm sure you have more important things to do than drive your manager to the airport, Clint. I'll call you when this T.V. thing is finalized."

As she turned away he caught her elbow and drew her back. "Damn it, Jordy. You haven't said one honest thing to me since I picked you up."

Her eyes narrowed. "Oh, you want honesty. All right." She sucked in her breath, and felt it burn her throat. She could feel all her rigid control slipping. "I'll give you honesty, Clint. Let's see if you can do the same. I got your message. Loud and clear. If you didn't see me alone soon, you'd go crazy." Her voice rose, the sarcasm biting. "I must have gone a little crazy myself. I rushed through all my work like a madwoman, and hurried to the studio, just to be with you. I got there around ten fifteen."

He looked puzzled. "Then why didn't I see you?"

Her voice rose higher, on a note of near hysteria. "I suppose because you were too busy looking at the little blonde on your arm."

She twisted herself free of his grasp. "You did have the decency to warn me right from the beginning. As you've said before, there are dozens of women willing to help you relax when the tension builds."

"My God! Chris! You're talking about Chris."

She turned away, feeling tears begin to blur her vision.

"Jordy, let me explain. Her car wouldn't start. She asked me for a ride home. I dropped her at her place. That's all. I tried to call you when I got home. There was no answer. And when I called the office number, I got that infernal machine."

Green eyes brimmed. "I'm glad to see you're such a gifted actor, Clint. Maybe while I'm in L.A. I can see about a good movie for you as well." She turned away. "Goodbye, Clint. Thanks for the lift."

He took two steps, caught her by the shoulder and twisted her to face him. "Why are you so willing to believe the worst? Why can't you trust me, Jordy?" His face was inches from hers. His breath was hot against her temple. "You're not going until we get this right between us."

She stared at the collar of his shirt, avoiding his eyes. Finally she lifted her gaze to his.

Her voice was choked. "I'm a good manager, Clint. I don't mind the crazy hours, or the chaos of life in the fast lane. I can fly to L.A., and hop off to New York, then hurry back to Nashville. It's all in a day's work." She licked her lips and turned away from the eyes that seemed to see beyond her words. "But I should have stuck with my original plan not to mix business with pleasure. Our personal relationship has to end. It just isn't right for either of us. I'm not strong enough for this."

She heard his sudden intake of breath. His voice lowered ominously. "I can't believe this. You think I'm lying about Chris?" His eyes narrowed; his nostrils flared in anger. "You listen to me, Jordy. We've reached a point in our relationship where we have to trust."

"You haven't been paying attention," she tossed out. "Our relationship is over, Clint. It was a mistake."

Catching her by the shoulders, he stared at her stricken face. His voice lowered. "You know what my lifestyle is, Jordy. You've known from the beginning. The fans, the women—they're a part of it. But I don't let them get into my personal life. And you can't either. Our relationship is never going to end."

He lowered his mouth to hers.

"The people..." she protested.

Crowds of passengers pushed past them. Cabs screeched to a halt at the curb. Porters loaded luggage. And in the midst of them, Jordan and Clint stood together, their gazes locked.

"I don't give a damn about the people."

His mouth closed over hers. A shaft of heat surged through her body, making her feel more alive than she had in days.

He held her firmly by the shoulders, drawing her so close she felt as one with him. She completely forgot the crowds of people. She thought only of the man who held her. She was achingly aware of the way their bodies fit perfectly together. His hard, muscular contours complemented her delicate softness.

The kiss was swift, heated, demanding, and when it ended, she felt breathless.

"When you get back from California, we'll continue this. In the meantime..." he brushed his lips over hers, sending a familiar tingle fluttering along her spine, "...carry this with you, Jordy, and know that I...care."

Her voice was a strangled whisper. "And I don't... care, Clint."

He released her, and she nearly swayed before turning away.

He stood beside his car, watching until she disappeared into the crowded terminal. Gradually he became aware of several bystanders' curious stares. With a sigh, he climbed into his car and headed back to the studio. It was going to be a long session.

Chapter Thirteen

Jordan lay beside the hotel pool, dozing in the late-morning sun. She was patiently adjusting to the fact that the business deals of southern California were often negotiated over lunch or dinner. Late dinner.

She had been here for five days, wheeling and dealing, and she had yet to meet one of the promoters or record company representatives before lunch. As she slathered on more lotion, she found herself wondering if any of them even bothered to go to their offices in the morning.

For her, of course, there were advantages other than the mere chance to sleep late and enjoy the pool. While the others were busy all day working, she had time to catch up on the latest record deals. More than enough time. She read the trades, phoned acquaintances from her days with the record company and swapped gossip. And over lunch and dinner, she listened. There was much more, she was discovering, to any deal than what was actually discussed. Often the things left unsaid were the deciding factors.

She knew the promoters were eager for the completion and release of Clint's latest album. His reputation was fueling a growing anticipation on the part of fans. And the promoters always listened to the public. The fans were the ones who spent big dollars for concert tickets.

"Jordan Hunter. Telephone call for Jordan Hunter."

A bellboy brought a cordless phone to her lounger when she responded to the page.

"This is Jordan Hunter."

"Jordy."

She caught her breath at the voice. She had tried, with no success, to keep him from invading her thoughts since she left Nashville. But Clint was the last person she thought of each night when she fell asleep. And his image was her first conscious thought each morning.

"Where are you, Jordy?"

"I'm out near the pool." She forced her voice to remain calm. "How's the weather there?"

"It's wonderful. The sun is shining. It's nearly eighty degrees."

"You're kidding."

He chuckled. "I'm not in Nashville. I'm at the front desk. I've been phoning your room since I signed the register. I'll be right there."

"You're..."

She stared at the phone. It had gone dead. Clint had already hung up.

A moment later he walked along the curving ribbon of concrete that circled the pool. She felt her heart turn over at the sight of him striding toward her. She tried to calm the pounding of her pulsebeat. It wasn't that she had missed him, she told herself sternly, it was only that she had needed to see a familiar face. But it was impossible to ignore the lump that formed in her throat at the sight of him. She steadied herself, taking in a deep breath.

With his hands shielding his eyes, he searched until he spotted her.

Jordan's skin was bronzed from her days in the sun. Her long hair was coiled on top of her head. Her white bikini was a counterpoint to her tan.

Clint's eyes narrowed perceptibly as his gaze slowly skimmed her.

"Do you always like to startle people like this?" she asked.

He gave her a lazy smile. "You're not taking phone calls these days. I figured the only way to talk to you was face-to-face."

"Does this mean you've finished the album?"

"Um-hmm. Yesterday. We had quite a celebration last night. I'm sorry you had to miss it."

She noted the tiny lines of fatigue around his eyes. "From the looks of you, it was quite a party."

He sat down on the adjoining chaise and faced her. "It would have been more fun if you were with me. I've missed you, Jordy."

"Well, I'm sure there were plenty of other...people to celebrate with."

He was studying her so closely, she looked away, avoiding his eyes. His voice remained calm, reasonable. "I want to meet the director who's going to handle the video for the album. Can you arrange it?"

"Thomas Marchand." She nodded. "Of course. You're in luck. He's back in town from his last assignment. I'll set something up. He'd prefer to do the filming here in Hollywood. The technicians are available. But he's willing to discuss the possibility of filming in Nashville, if you insist."

Clint was watching her eyes while she spoke. She avoided meeting his gaze.

"I haven't decided. We'll talk about it. That's one of the reasons I want to meet with him personally." He absently picked up the bottle of tanning lotion. "What's scheduled for tonight?"

She relaxed. Clint was going to make it easy for her. It was safer to stick to business.

"I have a dinner engagement with the representatives from B. and A. Promotions. They want to talk about the possibility of booking your show for a weekend if you decide to film the video out here. Tomorrow I have to drive to Burbank about the television appearance." She smiled. "This is a bonus. The B. and A. people will be thrilled to meet you. That is, if you'll join us."

"I was hoping we could spend the evening together."

She forced her voice to remain light. "We will. Together with about seven other people."

He ran a hand through his hair. "I think I'd better go up to my room and sleep. I came straight from the party to the airport. My head is complaining. Besides, my body's still on Nashville time."

"What's your room number?"

He gave her a level look. "The same as yours."

As he strolled away, she could only stare at his retreating figure. He had said that as calmly as if he were saying hello.

It took her several minutes to stuff her suntan lotion, towel and brush into the tote bag. She slipped oil-slick feet into her sandals, pulled on a terry wrap and hurried inside.

While she rode the elevator to her floor, she seethed inwardly. How dare he!

The elevator door swished open, and she nearly ran down the hallway to her room. Fumbling, she inserted the key in the lock and shoved the door open.

Inside, she glanced around the empty room, then walked to the bathroom. Clint stood in the shower, humming.

Angrily tossing her things on the bed, she paced the floor, feeling her fury building. He had gone too far. He had no right to assume that he could just move in, without even asking her what her feelings were on the subject.

She heard the water stop. A moment later, Clint strode from the bathroom, draped in a towel knotted low on his hips. She stared at the dark hair glistening on his chest. Then her gaze moved upward to his arms and shoulders, and she felt the faint stirring of a passion she was determined to deny.

Seeing her, he paused and ran a hand through his hair, which was damp and curling about his face. "I didn't realize you were in such a hurry to join me. I would have waited for you to wash my back."

"That isn't funny." She forced herself to keep her voice low. "And neither is this, Clint." Her hand indicated his luggage, which stood beside the bed.

"You don't like my suitcases?"

Her voice rose. "I don't like your underhanded tactics. You had no right to move in here."

"No right?"

"I'm here on business," she said, struggling to keep her temper under control.

"And what do you think I'm here for?" He moved several paces closer. Though she wanted to back up, she chose to stand and fight.

"I don't know, Clint. Maybe you'll tell me."

"I'm here to get a first-hand look at how you do business. In case you've forgotten, Jordy, you are my manager. That means I have a vested interest in how you do your job."

Her eyes narrowed. "Fair enough. And my job is to get you the best concert appearances, with the maximum publicity I can. And that's all."

His finger moved along her jaw, then dipped to trace the column of her throat.

"Meaning?" He watched her eyes as his finger trailed along the neckline of her robe, moving between her breasts, then lower, to her waist.

"Meaning I have no intention of sharing my room, or my bed, with you."

With one finger, he loosened the tie, allowing the robe to open. He allowed his gaze to roam slowly from her heaving breasts to the brief bikini pants, before once more meeting her eyes. No longer was her gaze cool or composed. He noted the smoldering fire that his simple touch had ignited.

He was undermining all her determination to keep control of the situation. Suddenly she was aware of the warm, steamy scent of him: lime soap, and the faintly musky fragrance of his shaving lotion. Little beads of water clung to his hair, glistening in the light. His lips were parted slightly in a half smile.

"Jordy." The husky quality of his voice should have sounded a warning bell.

He leaned closer, and she found herself drawn to him. With only his finger caressing her throat, he commanded her as if he were holding her with all his strength. Unresisting, she moved against him, needing to feel his flesh against hers.

His mouth closed over hers. His finger traced her eyebrow, the curve of her cheek. His other hand remained at his side.

The kiss was gentle, undemanding. Jordan found herself melting against him. How long had she yearned for a tender embrace? How long had she needed to be held? Her arms encircled his waist and reveled in the moist warmth of his skin. With a little moan, she deepened the kiss, until his hands slipped beneath the robe to draw her firmly against him.

Then the kiss became hot, searing. A surging need skyrocketed through her, shocking her with its intensity.

The robe slipped from her shoulders, and his hands undid the tie at her back. The top of her bikini drifted to the floor.

He bent his lips to her breast, and felt the nipple grow taut at his touch. His tongue, his lips, his fingertips brought pleasure that was almost pain.

With a little moan, he buried his mouth in a tangle of her hair.

Jordan moved in his arms, caught up in a passion that raged through her. She was losing herself again. Losing her control, her sense of who she was and what she wanted. Losing herself to a man who would use her.

She stiffened. "Don't, Clint."

He lifted his head. She had gone very still. He thought he could actually feel the cold seeping into her body.

"What's wrong, Jordy?"

She took a deep breath, struggling to control the tremors that still shook her.

"I want you to get your own room."

His eyes seemed to darken as he studied the tight line of her mouth.

"Why?"

"I..." She licked her lips, and could still taste his kiss. "I need some privacy. I have a lot of work to do. And having you around interferes with my concentration."

"Having you around improves my concentration." There was the warmth of humor in his eyes, in the curve of his mouth.

She ignored it. "I'm feeling crowded, Clint. I'm feeling . . . used."

"Used!" He gave her an incredulous look. The hands gripping her shoulders tightened.

She lifted her head higher, reminding herself not to listen to his words, but to think instead of the woman in his car that night at the studio, of all the women who watched him with adoring eyes.

He studied the angry thrust of her chin, the eyes that had turned to cold, hard emeralds. Without realizing it, his fingers pressed into the flesh of her shoulders, until she gasped in pain.

He stared at his hands, and for the first time realized what he had done. He turned away, clenching his fists at his sides.

Reaching for the phone, he dialed the front desk. "This is Clint Donner, in 523. I'd like another room. Send someone for my luggage." His voice hardened. "No. Ms. Hunter will remain here."

He turned back to her, watching as she drew the robe over her nakedness. It infuriated him to see the faint hint of a bruise on her shoulder.

"I'll be out of here as soon as I can dress." He strode to the bathroom, then paused and turned back to her. "I've never had to force myself on a woman, Jordy. All you had to do was tell me from the beginning how you felt. I never thought we were using each other. I thought what we shared was called love."

The knife in her heart twisted. Jordan slumped in a chair in the corner of the room, watching as Clint hurriedly dressed and closed his suitcase. Within a few minutes, a bellman arrived. Clint set the key to her room on the dresser, then turned to her. Without a word he nodded, and strode briskly from the room. When the door closed firmly behind him, Jordan sat, unmoving, listening to the silence. It had become a familiar sound. The sound of her constant companion.

Clint lit a cigarette and paced the floor of his room. This trip had been a desperate gamble. He had hoped that the time spent apart would ease whatever problem Jordy was facing.

He had explained about Chris. What more did Jordy want from him? Did she expect him to grovel? He was an entertainer, accustomed to women's inviting glances. He enjoyed it, and on stage, encouraged it. This innocent fantasizing of his fans was part of the job. But surely Jordy, of all people, should know that he didn't take it seriously?

He crushed out the cigarette and sat on the edge of the bed. Something had happened. Something that had devastated her. And she couldn't bring herself to tell him. The past hadn't been buried yet. It was still haunting her. He had no right to add to her burden. But it was tearing him apart to see her like this. He wanted to help her, to comfort her. But he was helpless. She was so damned independent she couldn't bring herself to confide in him.

He lay on the bed, trying to sleep. But thoughts of Jordy crowded his mind. There was no rest from them.

When she had come to him at the farm, it had been the most cherished gift he had ever received. She had given him so much. She had loved openly, freely, and with a passion that astounded him. His days and nights had been so full with Jordy, so carefree. And now that he had tasted her lovemaking, his life seemed even emptier than before. The loneliness was intolerable.

He sat up and lit another cigarette, then stared at it thoughtfully. Loving her was definitely bad for his health.

"Mr. Donner's room please."

Jordan listened to the ringing of the phone, and took a deep breath, forcing herself to remain calm.

"Yes?"

The sound of his voice had the shocking impact of ice water.

"Clint? Jordy. The B. and A. people are sending a limousine over in half an hour. I'll meet you at the front desk."

"Fine."

She hung up the phone and stared at it for a moment. Brief and businesslike. She would have to see that she kept it that way.

One of the first things Jordan had done when she'd arrived in Los Angeles was to shop. It would be sinful to visit a city filled with some of the finest designer boutiques in the world and not take advantage of it.

For dinner tonight, she chose a black silk dress with long tapered sleeves and a draped neckline. After carefully applying her makeup, she swept her long hair up into a dramatic knot, allowing tiny tendrils to drift about her cheeks and neck. She wore no jewelry except tiny pearl ear studs. The effect was dramatic. Slipping her feet into high, strappy sandals, she twirled in front of the mirror. Pleased with the results, she pulled on a trim fitting black velvet coat, picked up a small black evening bag and hurried to the elevators.

Clint was waiting at the front desk. Jordan tried not to stare, but she had never seen him dressed so formally. Wearing a dark, perfectly tailored suit, with a pale ivory shirt and carefully knotted silk tie, he could have been one of the many successful business executives standing about the lobby of this hotel. But even in these conservative clothes, Jordan noted the difference between Clint and all the others. There was an aura of complete confidence about him. And a hint of the rogue. The way he leaned his hip casually against the wall, one foot carelessly crossed over the other. The way his hands rested in his pockets, while his gaze swept the crowded lobby.

He straightened when he spotted her. "You look beautiful, Jordy."

He didn't smile, she noted, and the look in his eyes seemed guarded.

"Thank you. So do you, Clint."

That brought a half smile to his lips. His hand lightly brushed the small of her back as he guided her through the door of the lobby and out to the waiting limousine.

They sank into the plush interior.

"I bet the limousine rental agencies do a booming business in this town."

Jordan nodded her agreement. Everywhere she looked in Beverly Hills, there were limousines and exotic automobiles. This seemed to be a town of excesses.

The driver stopped at a small, exclusive restaurant. The doorman assisted them from the vehicle, and ushered them inside.

The lighting was dim, the atmosphere hushed and elegant. They were shown to a private booth, where seven men were talking quietly. As they approached, the conversation stopped, and all seven rose to their feet.

Jordan knew two of the men at the table. The others, investors with B. and A. and the company lawyers, were quickly introduced, before everyone was seated.

Robert Borden and Larry Allison, who headed B. and A. Promotions, were as different as two partners could be. Borden was short, paunchy, with a thatch of dark hair that encircled his bald head like a monk's crown. He spoke in rapid, gunfire bursts. His raucous laughter turned heads at the other tables.

Larry Allison was tall and tan, looking more like one of the celebrities he booked than a promoter. His pale suit was custom-tailored, a perfect foil for his perfect tan. His voice was deep, his speech precise. He looked as though he spent most of his time playing tennis, or lying around a pool.

"Boy, were we excited when J.D. called to say you were in town, Clint." Robert Borden's cheeks reddened as he spoke. "I mean, she's a great little manager, and all that, but it's still better to deal directly with the guy at the top. Know what I mean?"

Clint gave Borden an icy smile. "I have every confidence in my manager." He allowed his gaze to travel around the table, meeting their questioning glances, before adding, "I don't make a move without first asking her opinion. She's tough and shrewd and very capable."

In the ensuing silence, Larry Allison cleared his throat. "Yes. We certainly agree, Clint. May I call you Clint?"

At Clint's slight nod, he went on. "We've been promoting entertainers here in Los Angeles for the past five years now. Our events have showcased some of the finest talent in the world. I think you'll be pleased with what we have to offer."

He looked up as the waiter hovered. "Shall we order drinks first? How about a bottle of Chauteau Morganroth '68?" He glanced around the table, then smiled at the waiter. "And for me, Perrier." To the others he added, "Just trying to stay fit."

Jordan tried not to smile at the impatience she could sense in Clint.

"Now Clint," Larry Allison continued, "about what B. and A. can offer..."

"I'm sorry," Clint said, fighting to keep the sharp edge from his tone. "I'm afraid you'll have to present your package to my manager first. If Jordy approves, she'll pass it on for my approval."

Allison frowned. "I had hoped we could talk business tonight."

"You can talk all you want," Clint said goodnaturedly. "Just as long as you direct your comments to Ms. Hunter, and not directly to me. I'll just listen, if you don't mind."

Larry Allison seemed to really see Jordan for the first time. For one quiet moment he glanced at his lawyer, seated at the opposite end of the booth. Then, at the other man's slight nod, Allison turned on the charm.

"Certainly, Clint. I understand. Well, Ms. Hunter, may I call you Jordy?"

"No. I'd prefer J.D."

He lifted one eyebrow. "All right, J.D."

While he talked, Jordan sipped the excellent French wine and enjoyed her position. Thanks to Clint's quick thinking, these men now understood that Clint had not come here tonight because he wanted to take charge of the deal. They would still have to sell their promotional package to her first.

Dinner was an experience. Larry Allison insisted they try the truffles, a rare delicacy. Borden recommended the steak tartar, said to be the chef's specialty. One of the others suggested the hearts of palm salad. While she was trying to decide, Jordan happened to glance at Clint. He winked, and she grinned at him, while her heart beat wildly. How thankful she was to have him here with her tonight. Something about his quiet strength gave her confidence in herself. She was able to keep her perspective about this whole show, since that was really what this dinner was. These Hollywood pitchmen were trying to dazzle their country cousins.

The men indulged in after-dinner drinks, and Jordan ordered a Grand Marnier soufflé. It was heavenly, and she had to resist the urge to lean toward Clint and offer him a taste.

He seemed to sense her thoughts, and muttered, "You know you can't possibly eat all that. How about a few crumbs for a poor starving singer?"

She chuckled. "Okay, poor starving singer. Here."

She placed the spoon in his mouth, and he rolled his eyes heavenward.

"That stuff's terrific."

"Naturally. I have very good taste."

"I've noticed that about you." He leaned closer. "Are you almost ready to get out of here?"

"Not until I've finished my dessert."

"Make it fast. I can't take much more of this."

She sipped her coffee, then leaned back, enjoying the rumble of masculine conversation all about her.

When she thought Clint had reached the limits of his patience, she set down her napkin.

"Gentlemen, thank you for a lovely dinner. I'm afraid Clint and I will have to say good-night."

They shook hands all around, and strolled from the restaurant.

With the business of the evening concluded, she and Clint settled once more into the quiet interior of the limousine, to enjoy the ride back to their hotel. The evening was warm. She slipped off her velvet coat and laid it on the seat beside her.

"Truffles and Perrier." Clint chuckled in the darkness. "I think I'd rather have pizza and beer. Or..." he took her hand, and lifted it to his lips, "...spaghetti sauce made by that famous chef, Jordan Hunter."

Tiny threads of pleasure curled along her spine.

She lifted her face to him. "Thanks for making my job easier tonight, Clint."

"What did I do?"

She grinned at his mock innocence. In a sarcastic drawl, she chanted, "I never make a move unless my manager tells me. Why, poor dumb little ole me just wouldn't know how to deal in this big city without Ms. Hunter here to direct me."

Clint threw back his head in laughter. "Was it really that bad?"

"No. It was worse. I couldn't believe what I was hearing. But they bought it. And that's all that matters." Her voice lowered. "Thanks, Clint."

He opened her palm, and kissed it, then kissed each finger, before twining his hand in hers. It was a wonderful, sensual thing, to feel his lips on her fingertips. They sat silently, watching the neon lights of the Los Angeles freeway, until they arrived at their hotel.

"Pink stucco and flamingos. There's no place like home," Clint muttered as they walked through the lobby to the elevators.

Jordan carried her coat over her arm. There were several other people on the elevator. Though she and Clint didn't speak, she sensed what was on his mind. She shivered and reminded herself of her promise to remain aloof. Clint stood so close to her that they were touching. She felt the beginnings of a tingle along her spine. She glanced up to find him staring down at her, the hint of a smile on his lips. She tried to avoid his eyes, and found herself staring at his mouth. He had full, sensuous lips. As if he sensed her thoughts, he lowered his face, until it was just inches from hers. She turned her head, and he inhaled the wonderful wildflower scent that clung to her hair.

They remained silent until they stopped at Jordan's door. Clint held out his hand for her key, and she was immediately reminded of their argument earlier in the day. He had given her back her room key.

As he opened the door, she kept her eyes averted. "Thanks again, Clint. It was much easier tonight with you there."

"Then maybe you'd like me to stay and make things easier all night."

She hesitated for only a moment. "No. I don't mind being alone."

"I do."

His lips closed over hers before she could think. For a short time, the kiss was firm but undemanding. She started to pull back, but his arms came around her, pinning her to him. Her coat dropped from her arm to the floor. The kiss deepened. She could feel his control. He knew exactly what he was doing to her.

Without her volition, her arms came up around his neck. Her body molded itself to his.

He took the kiss even deeper, stealing her will to resist. She moaned softly, and ran her hands through his hair.

"Don't do this to me, Clint."

"What do you think it does to me?"

She could feel him losing his control now, trembling on the brink. His breath was hot against her cheek.

"I'm not letting you in my room."

"Would you like to join me in mine?"

She tried to push herself free, but his arms held her against him. "No."

His lips covered hers, stifling further protest. The kiss was no longer gentle, persuasive. Now there was possession in his kiss, and knowledge. The knowledge that the woman in his arms wasn't immune to his touch.

"I want you, Jordy."

She knew she should resist, but she no longer had the will. Her hands gripped his shoulders, as if needing his strength.

His fingers roamed her silk-clad back, sending hot sparks searing along her spine. As her hands twined about his neck, he slid his hands to her hips, drawing her firmly to him, making her achingly aware of his arousal.

His lips traced her jaw, then dipped to her throat. No longer able to resist his touch, she arched her neck. He moved his mouth lower, beneath the draped neckline of her dress. Her nipples were already taut, straining against the silken barrier.

She sighed, and he felt in that simple gesture her surrender. With a little moan, she drew him firmly to her.

He lifted his head to study her eyes, and froze. It was still there. The fear. The shadow of pain.

Clint wanted her. He wanted her so badly he felt he was wavering on the edge of sanity. He could take her now. He knew her so intimately, he knew just how to get a response from her. But for some reason, she had closed her heart to him. And until he could get her to open up, he had to wait. Because he wanted her love, not just her body. He was determined to have it all.

"Whatever has come between us, Jordy, it's still there. It's more than a blonde in my car. Much more. And I don't think you're ready to talk about it yet."

She lowered her head.

He took a step back. "You have to face the reality of my life-style. My public image has absolutely nothing to do with my private life. I would expect my manager to understand that fact better than anyone else. Apparently, you haven't come to terms with it yet. When you're ready to talk, I'm ready to listen." He paused. "Just knock on the door."

She blinked. "What door?"

He smiled, that lazy, pirate's smile she had come to know. "The door between our rooms."

"You're . . . ?" She glanced at the adjoining room.

"That's right." He shrugged. "Can I help it if that was the only room left?"

He heard her sigh in frustration. "I should have known."

He picked up her coat and handed it to her. Brushing her lips lightly with his, he lifted a stray strand of hair, sending a tingling sensation along her spine.

"Sleep well, Jordy." He turned. "And don't hesitate to knock. No matter how late the hour."

It took several moments before he heard the shutting of her door. He recognized the scraping sound that followed. She had dragged a chair in front of the connecting doors.

Chapter Fourteen

"Well, what did you think of Marchand?" Jordan sat beside Clint in the rented car, watching in admiration as he easily navigated the twists and turns of the Pacific Coast Highway.

Thomas Marchand's Malibu beach house had reflected the personality of its owner. Sandwiched precariously between ocean and mountains, its walls of glass offered spectacular views. It was a house of light and texture, and vivid flashes of color. The imagination of the director was obvious after even a brief glimpse of his surroundings.

"I'm impressed. Very professional. I liked his ideas for the video. In fact, I couldn't get over how similar our thoughts were. When I wrote that song, I saw nearly the same thing he described today." He slowed, downshifted, then took the next curve. "I think we'll work well together."

"Do you really think you'll be ready to film within two to three weeks?"

Clint glanced at her. "Why not? By then, we'll have completed the mixing. I'd like the first song from the album released as soon as possible. If we can follow that with a second, and the video..." He shrugged. "Timing's important, Jordy."

"I know. I just think you're pushing yourself too hard. It can all catch up with you."

He lifted an eyebrow. "I'm a big boy now, Jordy. I'll manage."

They merged into the Los Angeles Freeway and became swallowed up in a sea of cars. A thick blanket of smog hovered ominously just above the roofs of office buildings. Over the horizon it fanned out into an orange haze.

Swinging onto an exit ramp, they followed the signs to the Los Angeles International Airport and pulled up at a terminal.

Clint hauled his luggage from the trunk, then handed the car keys to Jordan.

"I wish you were coming with me," he said, watching her eyes.

She looked down. "I have at least two more days here. Then it's on to San Francisco. I should be back in a week."

"Be careful." He stood stiffly beside her. They had suddenly become awkward in each other's presence.

She stepped back, avoiding him with any part of her body. By mutual consent, they seemed to be feeling their way around the edges of their pain.

"Don't worry. I'm a big girl now, Clint."

He grinned. "Uh-huh. I think there's an echo around here. Well, goodbye Jordy." He bent and brushed his lips across her cheek, then stepped back a pace.

He stood watching until she drove away. Then he picked up his suitcase and strode inside the giant terminal.

He had seen the way her eyes clouded at his kiss. There was no denying that she was affected by his touch. Yet she had managed to hold him at arm's length—again.

When the 727 lifted from the runway, Clint stared down at the clogged highways. Somewhere in that teeming mass was Jordy. He was on his way to Nashville; she to San Francisco. Next week she'd return, and he would leave. Their lives were beginning to be ruled by schedules. There was little time for even a few stolen hours of privacy. Time. It was becoming his enemy. How was he going to reach her? How could he get her to open up to him?

When the No Smoking sign flashed off, he lit a cigarette and drew deeply. He leaned back and closed his eyes, allowing images of her to play through his mind like a movie reel. He thought again about what he had overheard at the farm the day Jordy had told his brother Danny about her marriage to Marty.

It was obvious, from what she'd said, that she had been terribly unhappy. But the truth was, she had said very little. He wondered what pain was buried beneath the cautious words. What had that bastard done to her, to cause such distrust? She was such a private person. She gave away nothing.

Clint stubbed out his cigarette and closed his eyes. What he needed was to get her out of his mind for a few blessed hours. There was only one way. He had to try to sleep.

"I can't believe all that hard work is finally behind us." Randy paced backstage, watching as some of the musicians warmed up.

"Weeks, months. They all run together when you've been swamped for time. But it's paid off. The critics have been kind. Now let's see how the audience reacts. They're the ones who matter." Clint jammed his hands into his pockets and watched while one of the stagehands did a microphone check.

A giant screen was suspended high above the stage, out of sight behind the curtain. The promoter had arranged it so that when the band broke into a particular song, the screen would drop down and show the video they had just completed.

Everyone was edgy. This was their first live performance since completing both album and video. Audience reaction to their songs was crucial. But until this concert was over, they had no idea what to expect on their upcoming tour.

Clint turned toward the door, his eyes nervously scanning the faces backstage.

"What do you want to do about the ballad?" Randy unconsciously tapped a wild rhythm on the back of a chair.

"I'd like to wait and gauge the audience reaction to a couple of other numbers first." Clint kept his gaze on the door.

Randy's face creased into a broad smile. "They're going to love us tonight, Clint. I have good vibes about this concert. But I don't know what to tell Spider about your ballad. Let's come up with some kind of a signal..."

Just then Jordan rushed through the doorway, obviously out of breath.

Clint shouldered his way past Randy. "Sorry, can it wait?"

Randy nodded, but Clint was already halfway across the room.

"Where the hell have you been?" Clint spoke roughly, then regretted it when he noted her flushed cheeks, the slightly breathless quality of her voice.

"Hailing a cab." She looked close to tears. "My rental car broke down. I had to leave it. Now I'll have to phone for another one."

"No problem. Go along with us on the bus for the rest of the tour. It's safer that way."

His offer both pleased and frightened her. It would be so much simpler to travel with the band. No worries about road maps and undependable cars. But she wasn't certain that she and Clint could survive such intimate confinement.

She glanced around the stage. "Did they deliver everything that was promised in the contract?"

Clint nodded. "So far I haven't found any problems. But the evening's young. A hundred things could go wrong before we're through."

She sensed his nervousness just below the surface. That was why he was so abrupt. The artist, the poet in him, always had doubts about his talents at a time like this. A big part of her job was stroking his ego, boosting his confidence. She knew that once he walked on stage and faced that audience, the nerves would disappear. The adrenaline would begin to pump. The performance would take over, assured and confident.

"Nothing is going to go wrong tonight. The crowd is a sellout. They'll love you. And the new songs are going to become their favorites as soon as they hear them." She strode past him to the stage. "Is the screen in position?"

He pointed. "Up there."

"Have they tested it?"

"I certainly hope so. We haven't had time for that." He scowled. "Where's Borden or Allison? That's their job. Aren't they supposed to be here?"

Jordan touched his arm. "Clint, let me worry about this. You just go out there and knock 'em dead."

She froze at the sight of three women in spangled jumpsuits getting into position on the stage. They were the additional backup singers Clint had hired for the album. One was a slender blonde. Jordan recognized her immediately. She was the woman in Clint's car that night.

"What are they doing here?"

Clint followed her glance. "The Lovenotes? After hearing them on the album, I invited them to do the opening concert. I think the sound of women's voices in the background added a lot to our new album sound."

"Do they have a contract?" Jordan fought to keep her voice even. He hadn't prepared her for this.

"Of course. I called Glen in Knoxville and asked him to draw up something right away."

"And you simply forgot to mention it to me."

"I didn't forget." He swore. "I thought you had enough to worry about."

Her voice had turned to ice. "How considerate of you. Will they be traveling on the bus with the band?"

"If they go over well with the audience. Otherwise, they'll be just a one-night stand. I want to see how the audience accepts them. After this concert, I'll make a decision."

"How . . . convenient."

She started to turn away. He caught her roughly by the shoulders and drew her firmly to him. "Now you're upset. I only wanted to spare you a little work, Jordy." At the strains of their opening song, his arms came around her. "Wish me luck."

"You know I do."

"Show me." His lips covered hers in a demanding kiss.

For a moment she froze. Then the familiar rush of heat flooded her veins, and she returned the kiss.

"Luck, Clint."

He studied her a moment, then brushed his lips lightly over hers. He released her and strode quickly to the stage.

She watched for long minutes before turning away to search for the promoters.

Jordan wanted to sit in the audience, among the people, to actually share their reactions. But there were too many little details demanding her attention. She had to settle for a view from backstage.

She had always thought Clint's eyes were the secret to his charisma. But now, watching him from the wings, she realized that he was dynamic from any angle. His hands, as he held the microphone, or strummed his guitar, drew her attention. She could imagine those hands holding her, touching her. She trembled. They were large, capable, with long tapered fingers. They should have been soft hands, a poet's hands, but they were work-roughened.

She studied his profile in the spotlight: tall, broad shouldered, with trim, narrow waist and hips. The jeans he wore were long, lean and just faded enough to look comfortable. Beneath these were elegant, hand-tooled leather boots.

The tweed jacket that he had worn on stage was already discarded. A soft, fawn-colored chamois-cloth shirt fitted him loosely, and the leather laces that crisscrossed the chest were untied. Between songs, she noted, he had already rolled up the sleeves.

The hot stage lights and the spotlights surrounded him with a glow of brilliance, turning his dark hair to a rich gleaming russet.

And his voice! As he broke into a sad song of unrequited love and broken hearts, his voice became a heart-wrenching, plaintive wail. On the next number, a teasing satire, he gave a low, throaty growl. His voice was a perfectly tuned instrument, which he played to perfection.

It was impossible to separate the voice from the man. His magnetism depended on both. He had great stage presence. He played to his audience, making them laugh, making them cry, charming them until they were on their feet, cheering.

When the band broke into the opening strains of the newly released song, Jordan held her breath. The screen dropped down on cue, stopping just above the heads of the band. The audience gasped with one voice. Then, as Clint began singing, the video was shown on the giant screen.

Her original choice of Thomas Marchand as director had been a wise move. The man was brilliant. And equally important, he had interpreted the song in the same way as its creator, Clint. While his haunting lyrics washed over the crowd, they watched the images on the screen. Jordan strained to glimpse faces in the audience. There were many in the front rows wiping tears from their eyes.

She wanted to let out a howl of joy. They were reacting. They were feeling. They were being touched by Clint's lovely words, and by the visual effects as well.

As the song ended, Jordan caught Clint's steady look. He winked, flashed her a quick smile, then turned to acknowledge the applause.

"Thank you. That song, 'Wildflower,' is from our new album. And it's dedicated to a special lady—our manager, Jordan Hunter."

Jordan stood backstage, awash in emotion. Wild-flower was her own special song. And she had never even guessed. What a beautiful gift Clint had given her.

She slumped against the wall, feeling her heartbeat slowly return to normal. She had been as caught up in the excitement as the audience. The applause continued to thunder, until Clint urged his band to stand and be acknowledged. For long minutes the audience cheered, refusing to stop until Clint held up his hand. Thanking them for their kind acceptance of his work, he suggested that they might like to hear a few more of the songs from the new album. The crowd thundered and cheered. It was several more minutes before they grew quiet enough to allow him to continue. He nodded to his piano player, who struck a single note. Clint picked it up, drew it out, then began softly strumming his guitar. The rest of the band joined him.

Jordan pressed her forehead to the cool wall, feeling the sting of tears. Her emotions were so close to the surface lately. She cried when she was happy. She had to fight back tears when she was sad. She refused to give in to the melancholy that enveloped her so often these days. But right now, with Clint's success assured, she gave in to the happy tears. She knew what this meant to him.

At the end of his performance, Clint strode off stage, to the sound of tremendous applause. Jordan handed him a towel, and he wiped his face before tossing it aside.

"You were fabulous!"

His eyes narrowed, studying her for a long moment.

She caught her breath. Could he read her mind? Did he know that at this moment, she wanted him almost desperately? His sheer physical presence on stage, the animal magnetism of him, touched her, aroused her as much as if he held her in his arms. Something contracted deep inside her, leaving her trembling.

The audience began chanting, calling his name. The chanting grew, until it roared through the concert hall like thunder.

Clint caught her arms. "Jordy," he breathed, "it was good."

Before she could respond, he drew her closer and kissed her deeply. Then he released her and strode once more on stage, to the wild adulation of the audience.

He did three encores. Each time, the audience refused to let him go, calling for more, chanting his name. Finally, after the last encore, Clint strolled from the stage, signaled his band that he was through, then caught Jordan's hand. Together they ran for the bus, which sat idling behind the concert hall. In that brief moment of privacy, he held her in his arms, then brought his lips to hers in a kiss of exquisite tenderness.

As the members of the band came aboard, Clint and Jordy passed around glasses of champagne.

"I'm so high, I don't need alcohol," their piano player shouted. "Did you hear that audience?"

Jordy nodded, feeling close to the clouds herself. It had been one of those rare electric performances, where the entertainer and the audience were in perfect harmony.

Clint refilled her glass. As they clinked glasses in a toast, he murmured, "Did you know that champagne was discovered by the monk, Dom Pérignon? When he first tasted it, he exclaimed, 'I'm drinking stars.'" Clint's voice was thick with emotion. "Tonight, I'm drinking stars, Jordy. With you." He seemed almost self-conscious about what he had revealed. "Do you think that may be a little too lofty for a country boy?"

The wonderful things he knew. Her eyes were shining. "Not at all. I think I like your fancy words, Mr. Donner. And I agree with the good monk. That's how I feel too."

She felt the sudden pull of desire. She had no doubt that tonight, in her aroused state, she would find herself in Clint's arms. And they would drink stars until the morning sunrise.

Randy entered the bus with a wide smile on his lips. Behind him walked the three female vocalists.

"What a night for a celebration." Randy poured champagne for the women, then drank lustily.

"J.D., I don't think you've met the Lovenotes." Randy introduced the women, saving the blonde for last. His voice held a note of appreciation as he said, "And this is Chris."

"Hello. You were very good tonight." It galled Jordan to make that admission. But Clint had been right to use them in the concert. The female voices definitely added to his sound.

"Thanks," Chris said, smiling. "This was a big boost for our careers."

She had a beautiful smile, Jordan realized. If they had met under other, more pleasant circumstances, she would have liked this ambitious young woman.

"How about it, Clint? Are you going to keep the Lovenotes on for the rest of the tour?" Randy was smiling down at the beautiful blond Chris, who stood shyly beside him.

Clint smiled at his friend indulgently. "We'd be crazy not to use them. Did you hear that audience reaction tonight?" He turned to Jordan. "Phone Glen and tell him to prepare a formal contract."

The three female singers shrieked and hugged each other.

For Jordan, all the joy of the evening was washed away by Clint's words. He hadn't even discussed this with her. He had simply ordered her to call his brother and have a contract drawn up.

"Will they be riding on the bus?" Jordan's tone was lifeless.

He shrugged. "I don't see why not. We have the room. It would be silly to have them follow in a separate vehicle."

Jordan felt suddenly cold. Had all this been arranged earlier, before Clint knew she would be aboard? Had this whole thing been planned so that he would have someone available to celebrate with?

She stood awkwardly. "Well. It was a great show. I'll see you tomorrow in San Diego."

"I thought you were riding on the bus." Clint's puzzled look slowly turned to angry disbelief as her words registered.

"Well you thought wrong. I...I've already phoned for another rental car."

"You shouldn't be driving alone at night."

She shook her head. "I need to arrive a little ahead of time to set up the next interviews. I want everything to go smoothly." Keeping her tone light, she added, "The car rental agency is delivering another vehicle in a little while. I'll be fine."

Randy seemed distracted by the woman beside him. "All right. See you tomorrow, J.D."

"Good night, Randy. Good night, everybody. You...you really were terrific." Jordan offered the musicians a too-bright smile.

Clint gave her a measured look. At the door of the bus, he stopped her. His voice was a low growl. "What's happened, Jordy?"

"Happened? Nothing's happened. I just..." She licked her lips. "I've just grown up. I find I like being on my own."

"A few minutes ago, I thought..."

"There you go. Thinking again." She shoved open the door. "I'll see you tomorrow, in San Diego."

There was a simmering anger in his eyes. She could actually see him fighting to control his temper.

He nodded toward the others. "This has something to do with the women, doesn't it?"

She tossed her head. "It has to do with independence, Clint. Mine and yours. We're both free to...do our own thing."

He caught her roughly by the arm, drawing her against him. She could feel the rage trembling through him.

"It isn't over, Jordy."

Her eyes widened. "What?"

"Our 'thing.'"

She pulled free of his grasp and bounded down the single step. She ran all the way from the bus to the deserted concert hall without stopping. She didn't want to pause, to look back, to think about what she was leaving.

As her headlights picked out the long ribbon of highway, Jordan thought about Clint.

What was it about him that forced her to continue to care about him even after seeing him with another woman? Her common sense told her that she was bound to get hurt. If she allowed herself to feel anything at all for him, it would all start again. The lies. The cheating. The pain. Only a fool goes back for second helpings of that.

He could be so gentle. But he could also be harsh. He could be thoughtful and considerate. She recalled the farmhouse filled with wildflowers, just because Clint knew she loved them. But he could also be careless of feelings, when he was distracted by the pressures of the business.

Clint Donner was a paradox: tough and tender, generous and inconsiderate, dreamy poet and pragmatic businessman. Maybe that was why she loved him. She loved the hint of the rogue in him, the storm beneath the calm surface.

Her heart thudded. Love. She should be wary of that term. Hadn't love led to heartbreak?

The songs in Clint's new album were all about love. A few were about unrequited love. But most of them were tender ballads of true love, and the lover of his dreams. Often, when he was singing, Jordan had the strangest feeling that he was singing them just to her. But a quick glance at the stage assured her that he was singing to the audience, the sea of faces turned up to him like sunflowers to the summer sun.

Don't flatter yourself, she thought angrily. Every woman in that audience thinks the songs are just for her.

Why had she really refused to ride on the bus tonight? She bit her lip. Maybe she was throwing Clint into the arms of that blonde. Maybe she was unconsciously testing him. The last time she had seen him with Chris, his excuse was that her car wouldn't start. Since then, she and her group had become part of the band. Now, they would be traveling and living intimately together.

Jordan knew that if she had gone with him, she would be certain that for tonight at least, he was hers alone. Certain, until the next time he was away from her.

She needed to get him out of her mind. Even her sleep was haunted by visions of Clint.

On a sudden impulse, Jordan turned off the highway and walked into a twenty-four-hour restaurant. Something hot. Then she would tackle the rest of the drive.

"Two months on the road is too long." Clint popped the top off a soft drink can, drank deeply and made a face. "This is the last time. From now on I'm telling Jordy to book us for just one month or less."

Randy smiled at his friend. "Where have I heard that before?"

"Well this time I mean it." He pointed the can at his piano player, sprawled across the adjoining seat. "Look at Spider. He spends hours on the road staring at that picture of his wife and baby. Then he snaps at everybody. We all need space."

"Hang in there, Clint." Randy stood and walked to the refrigerator. "One more week, and we'll be home."

"Sure. 'Til the next time."

Randy turned to study Clint. "What's happening to you, buddy? You're the one who talked me into this life years ago. You said you'd never get tired of hearing that applause."

Clint shrugged. "Maybe the years have a way of catching up."

"Uh-uh. It isn't that, Clint." Randy lowered his voice. "It's you and J.D. When we finish this tour, you'd better settle it once and for all."

Clint emptied the can, then crushed it before tossing it in a wastebasket. Randy watched as he strode toward his compartment at the rear of the bus. He knew Clint and J.D. hadn't been close since their days at the farm. But he didn't know why. Whatever it was, it was eating away at Clint, tearing him apart. And from the looks of her, J.D. wasn't faring any better. He shook his head. Love. Who could figure it out?

Chapter Fifteen

"Clint! I'm so glad you're home." Jordan's voice was an octave higher than normal. "A registered letter just came, notifying you that you've been nominated for Country Male Vocalist of the Year for your love song, 'Wildflowers.'"

There was a long silence on the other end of the phone. Jordan waited.

"Clint? Did you hear me?"

His voice was deeper than usual. "I heard you, Jordy. I guess I'm speechless. Give me a few minutes to let it sink in."

"Oh, Clint. I'm so happy for you. I'm so proud. All the work you did. All those years. All the bars, the state fairs, the concerts. And now this."

She could hear the smile in his voice. "Thanks, Jordy." He seemed to pull himself together. "Well, I've got to call the guys. The award is theirs as well."

"Yes. I'll let you go, Clint. And congratulations again."

"Jordy?"

"Yes?"

"How about dinner tonight? To celebrate."

"I . . . can't make it."

There was a moment of silence. "I see. All right. Goodbye, Jordy."

She hung up the phone and stared at it for long moments. The temptation to say yes had been so strong. It had been so long since they had been alone together. But her head won out over her heart. The separation was painful, but in the long run, much more sensible. In time, Clint would get the message and stop asking. And then the healing process could begin.

It was foolish to think that her heart would break just because Clint let her down. She had survived too many crises in her young life to think this one would be the last. But, she thought as she finished opening the mail, this was the worst. Clint had been her hero, her knight in shining armor, since she was thirteen. The knowledge that he might have shamelessly used her, filled his days and nights with her just to get inspiration for his songs, was like a knife in her heart. She had thought Clint was better than that. She paused in her work, staring at a beam of sunlight filtering through the smudged office windows. I have no right to blame him alone, she thought, trying to de-

fend him. After all, I was the one who went to him. All
he did was accept what I offered. And if he accepts the
same from other women as well, it's better that I
found out about it now, before the whole affair went
any further.

The phone rang, interrupting her thoughts. It was
the first of dozens of calls she would receive that day.
Once the media heard the news, the requests for interviews began pouring in. She was grateful for the
chance to be busy. That was the best way to avoid
feeling sorry for herself.

"J.D.?" She recognized Randy's voice. "Did you
hear the good news?"

"Yes. Isn't it wonderful?"

"The best. Listen, the guys in the band want to celebrate. We've decided to surprise Clint tonight with a
special party. You've got to be part of it, J.D."

She grinned. "I love surprises. What can I do?"

"Be ready at eight o'clock in your fanciest duds.
We're going to swing by and pick up Clint in the bus.
Then we'll drive to your place. From there we're go-
ing to the best restaurant in town."

"Oh, Randy. This sounds like fun. I'll be ready."

"Good. Eight o'clock, J.D."

She hung up and hurried through the office work.
By six o'clock, she had locked the office and headed
home for a shower.

Jordan had bought a beautiful dress in Los Angeles. Tonight would be the perfect opportunity to
show it off. Made of brilliant rose silk, it had very full
sleeves that buttoned at the wrist with a wide band of

smocked fabric. The smocking was repeated in the mandarin collar and the wide sash at her waist.

She pulled her hair back in a classic knot that gave her a pristine appearance.

I am not nervous, she told herself as she smeared her eye makeup. Her hands were actually trembling. She was all thumbs. What was wrong with her? It was just a celebration dinner. The entire band would be there. She wouldn't have a moment alone with Clint. Still her heart was pounding, and she had to rub her palms on a towel while she applied her makeup.

When she heard the knock on her door, she jumped. Scooping up a lacy shawl and a small bag, she opened the door. Clint stood in the doorway, looking wonderful in dark slacks and a suede jacket. The look he gave her was like a physical caress.

He watched her eyes, seeing the hesitation there, and cautioned himself to go slowly. She had avoided him for so long, he had nearly given up hoping they could ever talk this thing out. This might be the last chance to make things right between them. No matter what, he was determined not to frighten her, or push her too far. She mattered too much to him.

"You look . . . different, Jordy."

She blushed. "You're just not used to seeing me in a dress."

"No. It isn't that. The dress is beautiful. L.A.?"

She nodded.

"I think it's your hair. That prim and proper hairdo just doesn't fit the flaming dress." He smiled. "Fire and ice." He shook his head. "But somehow, it becomes you."

As she closed the door behind them, he murmured, "The guys in the band have cooked something up. They won't tell me where we're going. Do you know?"

She gave him a wicked smile. "Now really, Clint, do you expect me to give away our secret?"

"I didn't really think so. You're in on this, are you?"

"Randy dreamed it up. But we're all in on it. Come on."

With a light heart, he caught her hand. For a moment, she turned to him, feeling the familiar tingle at his touch. He gave her a bright smile. She returned it. Swinging their hands happily, they hurried toward the bus.

Inside, the celebration had already begun. Their latest album played on the stereo. Champagne was chilling on ice. The men and their wives or sweethearts moved all about the bus, laughing, chatting, in a holiday mood. It was strange to see the musicians in suits. Even on stage, most of them dressed in jeans and T-shirts.

Jordan spotted two of the Lovenotes, accompanied by handsome, eager young men. Instead of the glittering stage attire, they were dressed almost conservatively in simple silk dresses.

While Jordan was chatting with Spider and his wife, she saw Randy tap Clint on the shoulder and lead him back to his private compartment. When the door opened, Jordan could make out the figure of a woman. A blond woman. Chris.

The conversation going on around her became a blur of sound. Her throat constricted. While someone spoke, she nodded her head, unable to follow the conversation. Her mind was whirling with confusion.

How could Randy have been so callous? Why had he bothered to invite her, knowing Chris was going to be in Clint's compartment?

She turned, spilling champagne on the floor.

"J.D. Watch it." Spider caught her arm. "Hey. What's wrong? You're shaking."

He helped her to a seat. Touching her cheek, he said, "I don't get it. You've lost all your color, but your skin's on fire."

"I...think it's the motion of the bus. And too much champagne," she muttered. "I think I need some air."

"We'll be at the restaurant soon, J.D. Think you can hang on for a few minutes longer?"

Jordan nodded, too shaken to speak.

Spider frowned his concern. "You just sit there, J.D. Don't get up. From the looks of you, you'd fall."

Jordan pressed her hands to her burning cheeks. How was she going to be able to face Clint and Chris together?

At that moment, the compartment door opened, and a smiling Clint and Randy escorted Chris down the aisle of the bus. One glance at Jordan's face, and Clint was immediately at her side.

"What's wrong?"

Spider hurried over. "I think J.D. needs some air. Either she's suffering from motion sickness, or she's coming down with something."

Clint continued to study Jordan's face. "You were fine a few minutes ago."

He didn't miss the fact that she stared pointedly at Chris before saying, "I . . . just don't feel good, Clint. I think maybe I ought to go back home."

"I'm sorry you're sick, but I can't let you go. It won't be a celebration without you, Jordy."

She couldn't believe her ears. How could he calmly meet Chris in his compartment, and still pretend that he wanted Jordan with him?

"Please, Clint. Just let me go home," she whispered, hoping to avoid a confrontation.

"No." His voice hardened. With a dark look, he waved Spider away. "You're going to stay, Jordy. And that's final," he snapped, seeing her mouth open to protest.

"I'd better warn you, I may very well be sick right here in front of everybody."

"Go ahead."

For long moments, she stared at him. His jaw was so firmly clenched, she could almost hear the grinding of his teeth. Finally, she turned away.

"All right. Suit yourself. I'll stay. But don't blame me if I ruin everybody's celebration."

"You will have a good time," he said firmly. "If it kills you."

Her eyes narrowed. "We've just had some marvelous words of wisdom from our resident tyrant, Clint Donner." She met his dark look. "I'll have a simply marvelous time," she hissed through gritted teeth.

She missed the smile on his face as he turned away.

So this was it, she thought, while she forced herself to mingle. Tonight would be the final break. But as painful as it would be, at least she would finally step out of the limbo she had been in for so long. Tonight, she would have to smile while she watched Clint and Chris together. Tonight, he would find out just how strong she really was. She would not break down in front of him. She would smile if it killed her.

She had been good for Clint's career. But, she thought with sudden insight, he had been good for her, too. In these months, she had gained new self-respect. She knew now that she could make it alone. Whatever damage Marty had done to her ego, it hadn't been permanent. Oh, there were scars. There was still a lot of pain. But she would survive. Jordan tossed her head and lifted her chin higher, watching Clint joking with his friends. She would survive even the loss of Clint.

Chico's was a favorite restaurant with all the musicians. The owner led them to a private banquet room, where the tables had been arranged in a circle around the room. In the center stood a replica of their latest album. The music playing in the background was their music. Waiters scurried about, filling glasses, taking orders.

There were name tags, showing each person where to be seated. Jordan noted that she and Clint were seated alongside Chris and Randy. And for some reason, with each glass of champagne, Randy's smile grew wider.

Soon the wonderful aroma of spicy Mexican food filled the room, as dinner was served. For a while, the crowd became quiet as they concentrated on their meal. They became louder when coffee and dessert arrived, along with more champagne.

Randy tapped the side of his plate for attention.

"We're all here to help our good friend celebrate a special nomination."

Everyone applauded.

"And to pat ourselves on the back for a job well-done."

The crowd laughed.

Randy glanced around the room. "With J.D. here, we finally have the entire group together." There was a twinkle in his eye. "By the way, let's hear it for our manager, J.D. Here's to the human dynamo."

Amid whistles and cheers, she stood and acknowledged the praise, and swallowed down the lump that formed. For the first time, she became aware of just how much these friends meant to her. The work she did for all of them filled her hours, her days, her life.

"And now, let's hear it for our fearless leader." Randy smiled as he touched his friend's shoulder. "Clint, you took this good old boy along on the ride of my life. And I think all of you will agree with me..." He paused. "...I for one, hope the ride never ends."

A lusty cheer went up around the room. Clint stood, and was caught in a great bear hug by his best friend.

Clint held up his hands for silence.

"This is also a special night for my good friend Randy." With a mysterious smile, Clint added, "Earlier tonight, Randy shared some very good news with me." The crowd grew silent. "Now I'd like you all to hear it." He motioned to the couple beside him. "Randy and Chris have decided to get married."

There was a little gasp of surprise. Jordan wasn't certain if the others heard her. The room erupted into applause and cheering. A blushing Chris was hauled to her feet by Randy, and soundly kissed.

While the others continued to hoot and cheer, Clint leaned toward Jordan. "We have some talking to do."

"We do?" She couldn't fathom the look in his eyes.

"Um-hum. As soon as we get rid of the others." He caught her hand and hauled her to her feet. "Tell me, do you approve of Randy's choice of bride?"

Jordan flushed to the tips of her ears. "She seems nice. And Randy's happier than I've ever seen him. I'm glad for both of them."

"Then why not tell them?" He led her to the smiling couple, and Jordan hugged Randy.

"When did all this happen?" she asked the beaming drummer.

Chris stared at Randy, the love glowing in her eyes.

"I think it started for me the first time I saw her," Randy said.

"It was the same for me. He was so darn sweet. So helpful." Chris shook her head, as if still not believing. "Maybe being on the road together helped us decide so quickly. But even if we had been apart the whole time, I'd know he was the man for me."

Awkwardly, Jordan extended her hand. "Congratulations, Chris. I'm happy for you both."

Shyly, Chris accepted her hand. "Thank you. I know you and Randy are old friends. I hope we can be friends too, J.D."

Jordan smiled. "I know we will be."

"Do you know what Chris said when I worried that I was thirteen years older than her?" Randy looked at her with such tenderness, Jordan felt her throat constrict. "She said, that was a dumb thing to worry about, because all lovers are the same age."

Clint's gaze locked on Jordan.

They were nudged aside by several people who had hurried up to congratulate the happy couple.

When the party in the restaurant finally broke up, everyone trailed back to the bus. The owner of Chico's supplied them with coffee and additional desserts for the ride home.

Jordan sank down into a seat, feeling more confused than ever. There were too many things that needed sorting out. If Chris had loved Randy from the beginning, why had she gone home with Clint? She didn't, her inner voice taunted. He had been telling the truth from the beginning.

Jordan swallowed back the threat of tears. Had she imagined things that weren't really so? Had she been unconsciously blaming every man for Marty's weaknesses? Maybe Clint had been waiting for her to signal a desire for commitment. She sipped a cup of strong coffee and brooded. This night had only added to her confusion.

The bus ride seemed endless. For nearly an hour, Jordan dozed as they dropped off the members of the band. Now, glancing out the window, she realized that they had left Nashville far behind, and were traveling through rolling hills. She looked up to find Clint standing over her.

"Where are we?"

"Heading for the farm."

Her eyes widened. "Why?"

"Because I asked the driver to drop us there."

"Us."

He leaned closer. His voice was stern. "Us. You and me, Jordy. We're going to discuss a little business."

"I thought you never discussed business at the farm."

"I'm making an exception in your case."

She didn't like the tone of his voice.

"What if I say I don't want to go?"

"You have no choice, Jordy."

"You can't just..."

"I can. I already have." He ducked his head and pointed out the window. "In fact, we're here."

"How will we get back?"

Clint took her arm and led her out of the bus. "Who says we're going back?"

Jordan shivered, and he wrapped his arm around her.

"Clint, there are things..."

"I know. Plenty of things that need saying. That's why we're here. No interruptions, Jordy. No more misunderstandings. Just time to talk it out."

He unlocked the door and threw on the light switch. Soft light bathed the room, revealing the rows of books on the shelves, the gleaming hardwood floors.

Home, her heart whispered. She brushed the thought aside.

"I'll start a fire. Why don't you make some coffee?"

She nodded, feeling suddenly lost for words, and grateful for something to do.

In a little while, Jordan carried a tray of coffee and mugs to the living room. The sofa was drawn up in front of a roaring fire. Clint was standing, one foot on the hearth, his hands resting on the mantel, lost in thought. He straightened as she entered, and took the tray from her hands.

"Here, Jordy. Sit and warm yourself."

She perched on the edge of the seat, feeling extremely awkward.

He handed her a cup of coffee and poured one for himself. Standing by the fire, he studied her stiff posture.

"There are a number of things we have to talk over. But you're going to have to help me."

She nodded.

"Understand, I don't expect you to talk about your marriage to Marty. I don't need all the ugly details. But I get the feeling that the problems between us stem from the problems you had in your marriage." He set the cup down on the mantel and faced her. "Tell me."

She swallowed. It was time for honesty. It was long overdue. "Even before Marty died, I had decided that I had to grow stronger. I needed to be independent. I needed to know I could stand alone."

He nodded in understanding.

"Well, I guess part of the problem is, I spent so much time learning how to be independent, I forgot to deal with a few other problems that still linger from—those days."

"Such as?" His eyes narrowed.

"Such as trust. Maybe I was so drunk on independence, I forgot that you'd been on your own for a long time now. Maybe I wanted to keep you on a short leash." She shrugged. "I don't know, Clint. I thought..." she took a deep breath, "...you were seeing Chris on nights you weren't seeing me."

For a moment, they stared at each other across the distance, hearing only the crackle of fire, the hiss of the logs.

His tone was quiet, determined. "Jordy, I explained about Chris once. I didn't think I owed you any further explanation."

"I can understand that." Jordan's voice rose. "But if it isn't Chris, it will be someone else. Don't you see? There are so many women in your life, and I have no right to blame you for enjoying that fact."

His tone dropped. "So many women in my life." He shook his head. "Yes, I suppose there are a lot of women out there watching me. That's what sells records, Jordy. But I'd have to be a superhuman to be capable of what you're suggesting. Why didn't you ever just ask me if there was any other woman in my life?"

Her cup rattled against the saucer, and she quickly set it down. "How could I? I had my pride."

"Your pride!" He swore. "You let your pride keep us apart all these months?"

She stood, her eyes blazing. "That's all I had left."

He watched her head lift, her chin tremble. "Why shouldn't I believe the worst? During the years I was married it happened to me so often I stopped believing in dreams."

Now, finally, he knew. What he had always suspected was true. Clint felt a raging fury at the man who had hurt her so deeply, leaving her scarred and afraid to trust.

He caught her arm in a painful grip. "Jordy, I can't help what happened to you in the past. But I won't be blamed for it. Maybe some men can't be faithful. But I'll tell you this only once. Since you walked back into my life, there's been no other woman."

He saw her astonished look, and softened his tone. "Believe me, celibacy is a very tough road. I've been hell to live with."

"But I thought..."

"I know. Musicians, entertainers and their adoring fans. Sorry, Jordy. I'm not into that scene."

She glanced down. Her voice was nearly a whisper. "Years ago, when I first discovered I loved you, Clint, you left. You just turned your back on the farm and everyone on it, and walked away. Your father once said you were like quicksilver. Always on the move. He told me that you had to follow your dreams. Even if they took you from us forever. And if we loved you, we had to let you go completely." Her voice was nearly a whisper. "I thought maybe I should always be ready to let you go."

He stared at her bowed head. His tone softened. "That wasn't the whole truth. Jordy. Look at me."

She lifted her head.

He met her gaze for a moment, then thrust his hands deep into his pockets and took several steps, needing to put some distance between them.

"When you began blossoming into a woman, I couldn't keep my eyes off you. The whole family was aware of how I felt. Except you. You were so innocent, you didn't realize what was happening."

She shook her head in disbelief and tried to speak.

Clint held up a hand. "Pa took me aside. He understood what was happening. He warned me that he loved you like a daughter. And he wouldn't allow one of his sons to follow you around like a dog after a female in heat. He ordered me to put some distance between us."

She gasped. "Your own father ordered you to leave?"

"Joining the service was my idea. But he was right to want us apart. You were so young and innocent. And I might have dragged us both into something too strong to control." His voice deepened. "I left the farm, Jordy, not because I wanted to turn my back on my roots. I needed to leave, to broaden my horizon, the same way I had to read poetry and the classics. For the same reason I had to teach myself to talk like the announcers on radio."

She heard the soft drawl in his voice and smiled.

Clint spread his hands wide. "All of this shaped me. My granddaddy's religion, and my pa's fierce love of this land are reflected in my music. God, country, love. That's my music, Jordy. I'll never forget my roots."

He shrugged, and his eyes narrowed. "I suppose I thought I'd go away, give you some time to grow up and we'd get back together and live happily ever after."

"Happily ever after." Her voice nearly broke. "I believed in that once."

Clint was across the room in quick strides. He caught her by the shoulders. "I still believe in it."

She shook her head. "You were always a dreamer."

"And you were always such a tough little thing." A smile lit his eyes, but he kept his voice stern. "Because you're such an obstinate business woman, Jordy, I've brought you some contracts to look over."

How had he managed to change the subject so quickly? Her mind reeled as he opened a briefcase and spread out some papers on the table.

"Here. Study these proposals." He picked up his cup of coffee and walked to the fireplace. A hint of a smile curved his lips.

She glanced at the first. It was a legal document, drawn up by his brother Glen, for a three-year managerial contract, plus an option to renew.

"Three years?"

"You may want to do... other things after that."

She glanced at the salary.

"Aren't you being a little too generous?"

He shrugged expansively. "You need a new car."

She nodded. "With this salary, I could buy a whole fleet of cars."

She began to read the second. Her head shot up. "Clint, this paper says you're giving me the land adjacent to yours. Is that my parents' former property?"

He dug his hands in his pockets, affecting a casual attitude. But his eyes searched hers. "When Marty wanted to make a quick sale, I heard about it. I had Glen buy it. We've been holding it for you, Jordy. It was yours. It should always be yours. You deserve something of your own."

Something of her own. Something solid, something real and permanent. Through a mist of tears she ran to his arms. "How could you know? Oh, Clint. How could you know what this would mean to me?"

His arms came around her, holding her close to him. She drew her arms around his waist, pressing her face against his shoulder.

"This is the most wonderful surprise of my life. Thank you, Clint. Oh, how I love you."

He held her a little away, and stared down into her eyes. "Do you, Jordy? Do you really love me?"

"You know I do. I always have."

The look in his eyes softened. "Love has a price tag, Jordy. It's never free."

She wiped the tears with the back of her hand and stepped back a pace, startled. "What does that mean?"

"It means, I want a commitment, Jordy. My folks were good people who saw a homeless child. But from the moment I saw you, you were something special. It was as if a piece of myself had been missing. And you were that last piece of the puzzle. With you, I'm complete. Without you, Jordy, no matter how much success I achieve, my life is empty." He held up a third document. "Read this."

She read the paper quickly. Her head shot up. "This is a marriage contract."

He smiled.

"But..."

"I knew you would want to see it in writing. Is everything to your satisfaction?"

She wanted to laugh. She wanted to shout. Instead, she squared her shoulders and asked, "Would you like a lifetime guarantee or a renewable contract and options, Mr. Donner?''

He grinned. "Lady, this one's for a lifetime. I want to love you, cherish you, pick wildflowers with you, dedicate my songs to you."

"Oh, Mr. Donner. You do drive a hard bargain. But I think the terms are very fair."

He wrapped her in the warmth of his embrace. His voice was gruff. "Jordy, I've been so hungry to have you to myself. Those long nights on the road, the crowds, the interviews and the hype—I can take them all, as long as I know you'll always be there for me. I need you, Jordy. I want you forever in my life."

She placed her hand on his lips. "Don't tell me you need me, Clint. All my life someone's needed me. Now, I just want to be loved."

He reached up to remove the clip that held her hair in that prim knot. His eyes narrowed. He caught his breath, as it drifted down in silken waves. The look in his eyes was eloquent. His lips closed over hers in a kiss that left her in no doubt of his feelings. She felt the rush of heat, the familiar stirrings deep inside her.

His finger trailed her back, sending curls of pleasure along her spine. As his hand found the zipper of her dress, he paused. With his lips pressed to her throat, he murmured, "On second thought, I'd better carry you upstairs before I try to discover what sexy little thing you're wearing under that dress, or we'll never make it to the bedroom."

"I've always rather liked a cozy fire and a sofa. Besides," she said, laughing, "we won't even make it to the stairway." Her fingers fumbled with the buttons of his shirt.

He moaned and drew her down with him before bringing his mouth to hers.

The surge of desire was swift, overpowering.

Against her lips he growled, "Sensible. That's what I've always wanted in my life, Jordy. Someone sensible."